EDGE OF TIME

by
DAVID GRINNELL

ACE BOOKS, INC.
1120 Avenue of The Americas
New York, N.Y. 10036

For big E and little e,
whichever, relatively,
they may be. . .

CHAPTER ONE

WILLIAM BASSETT HAD JUST returned to his tractor when the dinosaurs appeared. Properly speaking, it was not the saurians he saw first, it was the jungle. He had just climbed onto the seat of his machine, preparatory to resuming his early spring plowing, when the entire back forty of his fields just up and vanished.

In its place was a wall of jungle, a belt of giant green growth that stretched as far as the eye could see. It was thick, lush as the most primitive primeval jungle could be. Bassett had an impression of thick greenery, not trees, but the raw violent green of tropical grass and fern grown to the height of mighty pines.

While he stared at this amazing forest wall, two beasts emerged from it, thrusting the thick treelike stalks aside like matchsticks. The beasts were, as the farmer recalled later, at last twelve feet tall. They had long horselike heads whose jaws were lined with sharply pointed teeth. These heads crowned long necks attached to bodies that sloped back like the trunks of giant kangaroos. They were a greenish blue, with yellow eyes and vicious fangs.

Bassett didn't examine them longer. He stepped on the gas, swung his tractor around, and headed for the house, disregarding the careful lines his plow had been making. Terrified, he dared not look back, expecting every moment to feel the breath of one of the monsters on his neck. When he reached the edge of the field, he cut his engine, jumped from the seat, and made a dash for the house.

3

There he turned around and looked. But nothing was following him. There were no giant lizards. There was no wall of primitive jungle. The back forty acres were in view again, and beyond them the gently wooded stretches of the valley, with the blue-purple line of the low mountains against the early afternoon sun.

Two boys from Cullenville, a small town about fifteen miles from Bassett's farm, started on a fishing expedition in the hills one Saturday morning, a week after the local newspapers had carried the story of the farmer's vision. They were not concerned with Bassett's strange experience; in fact it is quite probable they had not even heard about it. They were intent on trying to locate a small remote stream they had only vaguely heard about, which was reputed to be teeming with speckled trout. They had been up in the hills, wandering through the woods for the past three hours.

Although located in upstate New York, the country here was not especially good for farming land; the soil was thin and poor and barely covered wide rock strata, consequently this unproductive mountainous region was wild and sparsely settled. There were a couple of old iron mines somewhere back in the hills that had last been worked during the Revolution, but now abandoned for close onto two centuries. The locality was good for hunting, and not much else. The one thing you could be sure of was that no startling or spectacular news event ever seemed to occur in this sleepy, backwater scope of country.

But for these two boys—and later for an important segment of the population—an amazing surprise was in store. They emerged from a thick cluster of trees, clambered up a rocky slide that promised a view down and across to the next slope, the usual vista of old pines, stumps, broken rock, shale, and clumps of bushes. But what they saw this day was a long, sprawling valley, with sunlight streaming down into it; a valley that stretched endlessly on to the far horizon. The sight held them breathless, almost unable to believe their eyes.

In this valley, perhaps a mile or more away, stood a strange city like nothing the boys had ever seen or imagined. The houses were in the shape of beehives, made of stone and mortar, and were topped with glistening conical golden roofs. The boys saw people in this city, but they were too far away to be identified, and in the outskirts, workers were busy in the fields.

The boys stared at each other in amazement. Then, with one accord, they turned and dashed back through the woods, in search of someone to share their discovery.

When they returned about fifteen minutes later accompanied by a deputy game warden and a fisherman they had located, there was no trace of any city to be seen. There was only the familiar valley of rock and stumps and brushy hills. When they told their wild story in the town, needless to say, it was not believed. Nevertheless, it made the local paper.

Seated at a desk on the seventy-fourth floor of the Carlyle Publications Building, Warren Alton stared thoughtfully at a sheaf of news clipping before him. What, he wondered, was all this leading to? All around him the huge room hummed as the staff of the national picture weekly, *People*, worked feverishly at desks stacked high with papers and pictures to get out the next issue. But in contrast, Alton's desk was clear, save for the big folder of clippings. Just as Alton himself was relaxed and thoughtful in the midst of all this disciplined hurricane of activity.

Alton had just returned from the back mountains of Peru where he had gone for an important cover story on newly discovered Inca ruins, and which was the star feature of the current issue of the magazine.

Alton had come into the office that morning in response to his publisher's wish to give him a new assignment. As soon as he had sent in his name, Carlyle's secretary had come out and handed him the folder. "C.B. wants you to go through this at once. Then he wants to see you at eleven sharp." It was about ten now, and Alton, having read the news stories in the folder, was thinking about them, mentally digesting the information from the clippings.

After he'd read the story of Bassett's jungle, and the boys' valley city, he'd quickly gone through the rest of the clippings. The first thing he noticed was that all stories seemed to originate in the same general area upstate. The second thing was that they all dealt with different oddities.

There was the clipping that almost looked like a flying saucer story, and at first Alton thought it was. But it wasn't; not at all.

It was an account of something seen by a commercial airline pilot, co-pilot and passengers. They were in scheduled flight from Montreal to New York. Passing over a low mountainous region, about three-quarters of the way to La Guardia, they saw something ahead of them. It was definitely not a flying saucer. It was something stranger.

It was a group of three creatures flying through the air, one behind the other, on wide flapping wings. Each was about fifteen feet long, and their wings appeared like tremendous leathery affairs, as innocent of feathers as were their scale-covered bodies, colored brownish-red. They had small red birdlike heads with big scarlet crests. They were flying at about a hundred and eighty miles an hour, but the plane rapidly came up alongside and passed them.

The beasts took no heed of the man-made vehicle. They flapped along, unheeding, as the pilots and passengers gawped in amazement. The three flying monsters passed into a cloud the pilot had not previously noticed, and when he looked back both cloud and monsters had vanished, and the sky was clear.

On setting down at the airport the story had been told to reporters. The descriptions of the fourteen people who had seen the monsters tallied exactly. The observers were of varied ages, sexes, and occupations. They could not all have had hallucinations, and all at the same time. They all saw the same things.

But there were no such things.

Alton whistled softly to himself, when he had finished this and read through some of the signed depositions attached to the report. Something new in "unidentified flying objects" indeed! Except that everyone had clearly identified them. . . .

There were a couple dozen such clippings, no two quite alike. Several people had seen strange animals on roads, in fields. None as spectacular as the Bassett dinosaurs but still, strange beasts had been observed where none should be.

The population of one whole township had witnessed a volcanic eruption.

Northern lights, the newspaper sages called that particular vision. But the townspeople doubted the explanation.

About ten-thirty one night, just a week ago, someone in the town square had noticed a red glow in the eastern sky. He had looked and called others. There seemed to be the outline of a huge peak among the mountains. But the town knew those low, sprawling mountains. They harbored no giant Himalayan cone like this.

It was belching red and purple gases and they could see the puffs of vermilion steam and the streams of red-hot, molten lava tumbling down its sides. They called out their friends and their families and their neighbors. About two or three hundred people watched the fantastic display.

It had lasted about three minutes, this fantastic sight of a huge volcano in full eruption. They had seen blazing chunks of rock hurled into the ruddy sky in a gigantic fireworks display. And then they had seen the vision vanish as suddenly as it had appeared. One minute a blazing volcano; the next instant only the dark starry sky and the low line of their familiar wooded mountains.

Everyone agreed on several points. The descriptions were the same, as were also two other factors. No one had smelled smoke, and no one had heard any thunder or explosions.

That's why geologists, finding that even their most delicate instruments had not recorded such a phenomenon, had dismissed the story as merely an unusual visitation of the Aurora Borealis.

Alton was inclined to agree with the scientists. He had been in the Antarctic on one of his stories and he'd seen enough of auroras to know how startling they could be. But one thing remained in his mind: the town that had watched the volcano eruption had been in the same general area as the rest of the apparitions.

And there were other stories. All quite incredible, all sworn to be true by the various witnesses.

Alton pushed the folder of clippings aside and sat in thought. This was a curious sort of assignment. What was Carlyle dreaming up for him now? He glanced at his wrist watch. Time to see the chief.

C. B. Carlyle had built up his key magazine, *People,* until it was a rival to Luce's *life* and Cowles' *Look.* He had done this by ingenious promotion, steady drive, and an ability to guess in advance at some of the great news-breaks of the past decade. Somehow he'd made it part of the tradition of his magazine that his star reporters were on the spot before the big stories broke.

Carlyle's offices were plush and swank, but Carlyle himself was a man who had never lost the common approach. A stocky gray-haired executive who had himself been a newspaper reporter, a distribution manager, and even an advertising wizard, there were few things he hadn't familiarized himself with.

Carlyle got up from his desk when Alton walked in. The short gray publisher met the tall, younger reporter half way inside the room, and grasped his hand. "Glad to see you again, Alton. That Inca story was a fine job. Got a kick out of reading it myself."

As he turned to his desk and Alton seated himself before it, he felt a warm glow course through him. The Old Man knew that creative people like to have a good job appreciated. And it was a matter of professional pride, then, to try to do even better next time. "Thanks, Chief," he said. "I liked doing it. But what's this new business all about? I've gone through this file of clippings, but I can't see what you've got in mind."

C.B. leaned over, took the folder from Alton's hands, and riffled quickly through it. "Outlandish stuff, isn't it?" he smiled. "But there's a story in it."

"Oh, no doubt," said Alton composedly, "but it seems more like one for the summer silly season, rather than a presentation of serious work."

The publisher shook his head rapidly. "Now that's where I disagree. I think there's a really big story here. Maybe it's a crackpot one. But even crackpot stories sell copies. Remember the flying saucer rage? *Life* probably put that story in the money brackets when they took it seriously. You'll remember they devoted several pages to it, early in the game."

Alton nodded. C.B. went on: "As I see it, there's a new business developing here. Somewhere in these stories there's a notion that will startle all America, that will get people excited again, and give TV and newspapers a steady stream of headlines. I intend to be the first to break it. And I want you to take the next few days to work on it."

The reporter frowned. "Just where do I start? This thing seems to be a combination of all sorts of loose ends. There's nothing one can simply latch on to, like the idea of saucers in the sky. Here we have jungles and beasts, volcanoes and strange cities, and so forth. The only clue to the story line, or angle, that we have so far is that all these stories come from one general locality."

Carlyle leaned forward, clasping his hands on his desk. "Exactly! And I want you to go up to that area, Cullenville and the other places where these people have been seeing things, and look around. Talk to these people; see if you can shake their stories. If you can't shake 'em, see if you can link 'em. Or explain them.

"Maybe these folks are all drinking some sort of brew that's giving them hallucinations? Maybe some undiscovered narcotic plant, like Peyoti in the Southwest, is growing wild around there. Maybe the air's over-high in oxygen content and they're all a little ga-ga. Maybe they've got some sort of religious hysteria that gives them visions afterwards.

"But whatever it is, *there's got to be a cause!*"

"Hmmm," Alton said slowly. "Would you really like it if it turned out to be something they drank?"

Carlyle laughed. "Naturally, that would be of interest and we'd publish the story. But it wouldn't make a new fad that we could really cash in on. I'll publish whatever you find, but I've got a hunch it's going to be something tougher to pin down than the suggestions I just threw off. I'd like to see a story that will start the rest of the country buzzing, and start some wild stories from other places. I'd like to see volcanoes pop up in Kansas and dinosaurs in Oregon. A Florida housewife spot cities in the swamps. In short, it would be nice to have another U.F.O. thing start from your article.

"But you know *People* is an honest magazine, Alton. If there's a sane solution, we're not going to fake it. But personally I think that this sort of thing is going to spread, and I want the story first from the original sources."

"Okay, chief," said Alton. "When do you want me to start?"

The publisher smiled. "I think you'd better start at once—this afternoon, if possible. Take a photographer with you. You can get pictures of the places and characters in these news stories and any other stories around that didn't make the wires. Tell Gardner to assign you someone."

Back at his desk, he called Gardner, manager of the photography department, and relayed Carlyle's instructions. He said he wanted the photographer ready to leave about one-thirty, and to meet him at his desk. Meanwhile Alton would have his lunch, pack a few things, and get his own car out of the garage. He'd drive upstate that afternoon.

Gardner grumbled as usual. All his good men were on assignment. Carlyle was wasting talent on a fool project. Well, he'd find someone.

CHAPTER TWO

WHEN WARREN ALTON returned to the office a little before two, his three-year-old Dodge parked in the building garage, his bags—which he had never really had time to unpack—stowed away, he strode up to his desk expecting to find his photographer ready and waiting.

There was no man near his desk, but a girl was sitting tilted back in his seat, reading a movie fan magazine. Warren's first impression was of a head of glistening black hair, and a pair of guileless green eyes as the girl looked up at his approach. The eyes widened and the mouth smiled.

Warren stood and looked at her. "Yes?" he said. "Anything I can do for you?"

The girl nodded. "I guess so. That is, Mr. Gardner said I'm to go with you on an assignment. You must be Warren Alton, the writer. I liked the story of yours in the latest issue. . . ."

Alton shook his head to clear it. "I don't understand," he said. "I was told that a photographer was supposed to meet me here."

"Oh," she said in an untroubled voice, "that's me. I'm the photographer. See." She pointed at the floor next to the desk.

Warren's eyes followed the finger to what was indisputably a Speed Graphic, a candid camera of some sort, a large leather shoulder kit of equipment, and a red-leather overnight bag. "My name's Margaret McElroy. I started working for *People* only last week, and you're my first big job. My uncle, Sam Murray—he's Eastern circulation manager—told me a lot about you, Mr. Alton. You can call me Marge, all my friends do. Mind if I call you Warren? It's so much more friendly and informal."

"Oh, *no!*" Warren gasped. "Excuse me a minute." He grabbed across the desk, unhooked the phone and hollered at the switchboard to connect him with Gardner.

It was a futile call. Gardner, head of the photographic department was adamant. Yes, he knew it was embarrassing to send a girl unescorted with him, but yes, Miss McElroy was quite a good photographer—she's won several contests in amateur and semi-pro status. No, he really didn't have anyone else available. Well, yes; maybe there'd been a little string-pulling from the circulation department, "but you know how it is, Warren."

Warren slammed the receiver down, glared at the girl. "Well, let's go! My car's in the garage."

He picked up her overnight bag, while Marge gathered

her cameras and equipment. Together they went down, piled her stuff away, and headed for the highways.

For the first two hours, Warren uttered no word. Marge, who had plunked herself into the front seat next to him, simply watched the scenery, remarking on odd sights.

By the time they had passed Poughkeepsie, Warren was beginning to relax. They stopped off for coffee and chatted a bit, and by the time they had reached the general area of Coningo County, they were on a working acquaintance.

It was after five when Warren drove on to Cullenville, and drew up before a motel just outside of town. "Looks like a good place to make our headquarters," he said.

"Yes," agreed the girl. "Nice. I wonder if they have a swimming pool."

"I don't know, and besides, we're going to be on the ball. The whole idea is, Miss McElroy, to get this story wrapped up as fast as possible, and then get back to New York. After that, you may head for Coney Island, Rockaway, or wherever you like to swim. But for me, I'll look forward to an air-conditioned apartment, relaxing in a cool tub, with a chilled planter's punch and a good book close at hand."

She smiled. She had a nice smile, Warren decided rather grudgingly. "Doesn't sound so bad, at that," she admitted. "Maybe magazine writers aren't all as crazy as I've heard they were."

They got out, walked to the office, rented adjoining cabins, parked their luggage therein. When they met again to go for supper in town, her first words were, "Besides they don't have a pool anyway."

He nodded. She added, "How about calling me Marge? We gotta get along for the next few days. What do your friends call you?"

Warren followed the girl into the car. "Mostly just Warren, I guess."

Next morning Warren banged on her door bright and

early. He knocked several times. Finally a yawning voice called for him to desist. "Rise and shine," he called. "Up and about. We've got work to do!"

"Say," she said finally, poking her head out. "It's only seven o'clock. What's the idea?"

He smiled at her sweetly. "When you're on an assignment with me, Marge, we start early. So get dressed pronto. Get the show on the road."

A little later, as they were eating breakfast in the main street of Cullenville, Marge, now trim and awake, asked where they were to start.

"I think the first person to see is William Bassett," he replied. "It seems to me that he was the first to see something. If there's anything at all fishy about these experiences, it would logically start with him. So we're going out to his farm. That's another reason for an early start. Farmers rise with the sun, you know."

Bassett's place was back in the foothills. It was a fair-sized farm for the neighborhood, but parts of it were rather rocky and not too productive.

Inquiring at the rambling farmhouse, they located Bassett in the fields. He turned out to be a heavy-set man in his forties, intelligent with a fairly good education.

At first Bassett was annoyed. "I've spoken to reporters several times," he said, "and I'm getting a bit tired of it. Most of them don't believe me. Fact is, there isn't anything but my word for it."

Warren Alton, however, had probably a good deal more skill than the small-town reporters who had seen him before. He easily won the farmer's confidence and drew him out. Marge turned out to be quite helpful. It seemed that Bassett was not at all averse to having his picture appear in the big slick pages of *People*.

He posed for her on the seat of his tractor. He led the two of them to the same spot where he had seen his jungle

appear, and the two beasts come out. He described them a-
gain, and answered questions.

Warren was taking it all down carefully. He looked into
the brief case he had brought with him and extracted a small
book. Opening it, he showed some pages in it to Bassett.
The book was about dinosaurs and other animals of pre-
historic times, with drawings of several kinds of these
monster lizards.

Bassett took the book and studied it. "Well, now, I'd say
that the creatures I saw were certainly like these but I don't
see any pictures that were *exactly* like them. Now these
fellows . . ." and he described them again.

His description tallied with his original news account.
He had not taken advantage of the time passage to em-
broider the yarn. That, thought Warren, was to his credit.

Warren wandered around the scene for a while, looking
over the ground, examining the underbrush. "You won't find
no footprints, mister," said Bassett. "There weren't any."

Warren merely nodded, went on looking anyway. Finally
they went back to the house, leaving Bassett working again
in the fields. In the house, Warren talked briefly with the
farmer's wife, then the two took their leave.

"So did you find out anything, Warry?" said Marge as
they headed back to town. "Maybe he was drunk, huh?"

"No, no," said Warren, shaking his head. "First, let's keep
it plain Warren. And I'm pretty sure that Bassett was on
the level. That was why I went back to the house. But it's the
home of a sober, church-going man, to judge from his wife.
I was looking for some kind of weeds around his back fields
when he thought I was hunting footprints. But I saw nothing
suspicious."

Back in Cullenville the quest went on. Warren and
Marge visited the local policeman, had a chat with him,
looked in on the hay-and-feed store and talked about Bassett,
took some photos of the main street.

Next they looked up one of the two boys who had seen the strange city. He was at school, but his mother was very friendly. Her son, she said, was honest, was not in the habit of making up tall tales. She couldn't account for the thing he said he saw, but insisted that he must have been honest about it. She invited them to wait for the boy to return home for lunch—to join in the meal.

They took the invitation. Afterwards, as they returned to their car, Marge said, "I can't figure it. How could he have seen a whole city where it wasn't? And such a funny city, too."

Warren was thoughtful. "It seems to me that these people are sincere. The primitive city the boys described sounds a little like some sort of African native villages I've seen. Now I wonder if it's possible for a mirage to appear halfway around the world?

"You see, if we could figure out that, for some reason, this locality attracted mirages of some sort, then the other details could simply be mistaken. There are African tribes who make huts of a beehive shape. Of course they wouldn't be golden and all the other details the boys saw, but maybe in the light, and maybe in the hurry, the rest of the stuff got into the story.

"Same thing with Bassett's jungle. If we could imagine an African veldt scene suddenly reflected by a mirage onto his farm, he could mistake say a giraffe or a pair of elephants for something more like dinosaurs."

"Yeah, but how could a mirage go so far, and how come it's only around here they see 'em?" said Marge.

"Ah," said Warren, "there's the rub, as Hamlet would say. The six-dollar-and-forty-cent question."

They spent the afternoon on an active roundup of other persons noted in the various stories. They spoke to many people who had seen the volcano that time, and their stories checked with remarkable consistency. They snooped around in an effort to locate some signs of moonshining or dope, but no signs could be found. As far as rural communities went, Coningo County was remarkably clean.

It was a lovely locality. The fields were green and rolling, the houses fairly well kept and the roads wooded. The central and eastern section of the county was heavily mountainous, with the rolling, darkly wooded and often steep mountains of the type found in the general belt of the Appalachians and Green Mountains.

They spent the next day in the same way. Again driving around the lovely mountains, looking in on isolated farms, talking to people in small crossroads hamlets. The visions all these people had seen were varied, yet marked by the fact that the viewers were insistent on their integrity. They turned up a number of accounts that had never made their way into the papers. And they turned up some corroborative evidence.

They found several people who had seen winged dragons of the same type as those spotted from the airliner. In fact it would seem that they were the same dragons, for two of the persons remembered an airplane passing overhead at the same time.

They found a number who had seen beasts of various odd kinds, and one who claimed he saw a number of queer lights in the sky at the dark of night.

By the morning of the third day, they had accumulated quite a bit of material, many photographs of people and places. "But not a darn picture of a monster or a flying whatsit," frowned Marge over breakfast.

They were eating at a little roadside place near their motel. Warren had been shuffling through his notes as they ate, trying to determine his next point of attack. He nodded, thumbing through his notebook. "I didn't think we'd be that lucky, and we weren't. Can't conjure up a vision just to order."

Marge nodded. "Yeah, but I was ready for it." She tapped a little candid camera she had slung around her neck. "This little .35 milli was ready to click on sight. Never took a shot with it, though. I only need ten seconds, that's all."

Warren put his notebook aside, took out their road map again. "I have an idea," he said, looking at the map. "Come on back to my cabin. I think I can figure this out."

They returned to his cabin, where he spread the map out on the writing desk. "Get a pencil," he directed the girl, "and place an X on every location I call out."

She bent over the map. He sat on the bed and went through his notes, calling out the various towns and places where they had been. When he was done, she had about thirty such marks on the map.

He looked over it. There was one thing apparent immediately. "They're all in the same general neighborhood," said Marge, anticipating his observation.

"Yes, and that's significant if we can only find out why," said the reporter. "Note that the farthest points can't be more than about forty miles apart, with the rest clustered in between. The whole area in which these visions have been occurring can be inclosed in a circle—" here he penciled it in around the area "—not more than forty miles in diameter."

"That's right. So maybe we ought to concentrate on the other places in the circle we haven't heard from, and maybe turn up some new stories."

Warren nodded. "That isn't a bad idea, and I think we would get some new ones, too. But that wasn't what I had in mind. What I want to find out is just where the center of this—disturbance—is."

He got out a ruler and started to draw lines connecting the farthest opposing points. When he was done the map was criss-crossed with lines. But at once they could see that they did indeed have a central radiant.

The lines kept crossing each other at almost the same spot.

They both bent over the map. "Seems to be a hamlet near there. Let's see. . . . Bloomfield Corners. That, we could call the 'vision center.' Can't be much more than a whistle stop," remarked Warren.

"We passed near there yesterday," said Marge. "That was up in the mountains."

"And that's where we're heading for today," said Warren. "It's the center of the area where these things take place. They must have seen things there—and maybe we can get at the origin of this thing, if it has one. Pack your stuff. Bloomfield Corners is our new headquarters."

"I guess if we hang around there long enough, we ought to see something ourselves," said Marge. "That's okay with me, even if we pitch a tent in the grass—I wanna get a shot of one of those monsters—I'll bet it would make the cover."

"Hope so," Warren laughed. They packed and piled into the Dodge and set off again.

In about half an hour they were driving along the winding back country road when they came to a dilapidated crossroads store and a paint-peeling old farmhouse. A weatherbeaten sign across the front of the store said "Bloomfield Corners" and an old gas pump indicated that this was it. Just beyond the two old structures the road narrowed and headed off steeply into the mountains, which at this point towered abruptly upward in a steep slope of pines and rocks.

They pulled the car up, got out, and entered the general store.

CHAPTER THREE

IT WAS DARKISH inside the store and for a moment or two they had to adjust their eyes. There was a counter running along one side, behind which were shelves piled high with cans of groceries. On the other side, other shelves and barrels held assortments of goods of all types, candy, overalls, etc. In one corner, there was a grated window, a series of mail boxes, and the sign of a U. S. Post Office.

An old man came out from a room somewhere in the rear and greeted them. "Is there anything I can do for you?"

Warren looked to him, went to meet him. "Perhaps you can help us. We're doing a little research for the magazine *People*."

The old man nodded. "Oh," he said, "you must be that reporter and the girl that folks been telling me about. Looking into those yarns about the critters and things, eh?"

"That's right," said Warren, "and I wonder if you know anyone around here who has anything to contribute to the stories."

"Wal," said the old storekeeper, "you've come to the right place. I've seen some humdingers in the past few weeks, yessirree!" He blinked as one of Marge's flash bulbs popped.

It took a little while before he got to talking. He had drawn up an old chair, while Warren sat on an apple crate and Marge perched herself on top of the counter and started examining a copy of a recent movie magazine from the rack nearby.

The old man, it seems, had indeed witnessed a number of things—as had, according to him, his wife and one of the neighbors down the road. There was, he said, "a stampede of crazy critters down the road in the dead of night— only they was all lit up like the sun was shining just on them. My wife said they was ghost cattle, but me, I just watched them from the window. They was four-legged all right, and they had horns, but they weren't no cattle I ever seen. They had slight humps, and bushy tails, and were sort of lean, low-slung and gaunt. They were running mad like they was something chasing them, but we never saw what. Must have been hundreds of them come along in only a half a minute, and then—*bam!*—they all just blanked out."

"No footprints on the road? Did they make any noises?" asked Warren quickly.

The old man shook his head. "Nope. Looked at the road next day; no sign of anything. And didn't hear nary a sound. Figure maybe they was ghost things. . . ."

Warren waited patiently while the old man ruminated. Then the storekeeper remembered seeing, "a range of mountains over where they shouldn't be, with trees and landslides and all. And once I saw a lake right across the road, with the Smithson's house just vanished and the blue water shining there. Neither sight lasted more than a few blinks, but they sure looked real."

Warren noted all these stories. He had guessed right, he thought, in figuring that this spot was near the intensity center of the visions. But he remembered that while Bloomfield Corners was near, it was still just a hairbreadth away from the exact center of his map. The exact center was apparently somewhere up the mountain that rose behind the store.

"Anybody live up this mountain?" he asked the storekeeper.

The old man nodded. "Used to be a couple summer lodges up on old Thunderhook, but mostly the folks have just left them go. One of 'em's being used, though. Bunch of fellers working on something. University men, I guess."

Warren sat up sharply. "University men? How can you tell?"

"Why, that's easy," said the storekeeper. "I'm the postmaster here, and I see they get letters addressed to Doctor So-and-So from some big colleges."

"Do you suppose we can go up and pay these gentlemen a visit?" Warren asked.

The old man shook his head. "I doubt if they'd like it.

They don't seem to exactly care for visitors—least-ways they rarely get them. Road up Thunderhook is marked private these days. Seems they bought up all the places along the old road."

"Where's the old road start? I'd like to go up and see for myself."

The storekeeper got up, went to the door. He pointed up the road. "Go up about two hundred feet, and you'll see a narrow old dirt road branch off to your right. That'll take you up the mountain along the Old Hook Road, which runs right up Thunderhook. It's not paved, but I guess it's passable. Drive careful, there's some sharp spots and turns."

Marge put down her magazine and got to her feet. "We going up?"

Warren nodded. "Let's try." The two piled into the car. Warren started the engine; the car began to roll.

As he drew away from the general store, another car came down the road from the direction of Cullenville. It was a black-painted station wagon, and it drew up sharply in front of the Bloomfield Corners store. Warren slowed his car, looking for the turn-off up the mountain and at the same time keeping an eye on his rear mirror where he could see the other car.

He saw a man leap from the driver's seat of the car and hurry into the store. He got a brief impression of a hard-faced man, big and muscular, wearing a short Navy-style pea jacket. He turned to concentrate on the road.

The old road up the mountain opened abruptly onto the side of the road they were traveling. He swerved the car, turned off the paved highway onto the dirt-and-rock road which seemed narrow enough for only one car. As he turned, he glanced back.

He got a glimpse of the hard-faced man dashing out of the Bloomfield Corners store and jumping into the seat of his

station wagon. He saw the wagon start forward in a jerk
of gears and he heard the horn sounding violently.

Warren looked ahead at his own narrow road. It would
soon head upward at an alarmingly steep grade. He stepped
on the gas as much as he dared, shot along the road and began to climb up old Thunderhook. Behind him he heard the
insistent horn of the station wagon.

The road was very narrow, heavily rutted, and never
meant for speeding. It wound in and around big slides of
rock, skirted big stands of trees, through which they could
see only the dense underbrush on the steep slope of the
mountain side.

Warren kept his foot on the gas, swerving the car by
sheer instinct around blind turns, up high gradients, over
bends. Marge sat glued in her seat next to him, watching the
road with the same dread fascination people get while riding
a roller coaster or tearing down an icy hill in a toboggan.

"Slow down," she finally got out, "before we get killed.
If we meet a car coming down, we're done for."

Warren gritted his teeth and kept up the pace. Finally
he managed to get out, "I'm going to find out about this
business, and I'm darn sure the answer's up here somewhere. It all adds up."

He kept the mad pace. Around corners, traveling almost
blind, between thick walls of green on each side. Often it
seemed the forest was directly in their path until the narrow
dirt road sharply swerved. The car had good springs, or
they would have been jolted into the thick undergrowth a-
longside.

Marge was finally able to take her eyes from the terrifying
sight of the road in front to look behind. She shuddered,
seeing the steep grades they had climbed. For an instant
there was a clear long stretch behind them and she saw
the front of the station wagon come around a bend below. Its
horn sounded again.

"He's still following us," she gasped, turning around to fix the road ahead.

"I thought he would," muttered Warren, twisting the wheel violently to avoid a low overhanging branch. "He's part of this. But this still isn't posted as a private road. I'm not stopping."

Just then they came out momentarily on a wide, almost level stretch. There was a sign nailed to a tree. Marge read it aloud as they roared past. "It says 'No Trespassing,' she told Warren. "See, it *is* a private road."

"Uh-uh," he said. "I didn't see any such sign. . . . Hold tight!" The car made a lurching swerve around an out-cropping of rock while climbing at an angle.

Marge recovered herself a little. Apparently once Warren was hot on the trail of a story, nothing short of sudden death would stop him—if that. She decided she might as well play the game, too. She unsnapped the case of the little camera slung about her neck, adjusted it with one hand while holding on to the jumping, jolting seat. Then she deftly twisted around and aimed the camera out the rear window.

In a few more seconds the pursuing station wagon made a momentary appearance, and she snapped it. "At least when we're either in jail or in the morgue," she remarked, "*People* can run a picture of our last moments along here."

She turned and shot a second view of a particularly fearful section of the road ahead. To one side the narrow road was skirting an almost sheer drop hundreds of feet deep, with tree-tops far below looking like a green carpet. To the other side, a wall of jagged rock thrust abruptly toward the sky.

They rounded a turn, tore up a straight section with another turn coming up a hundred feet ahead. The honking of the station wagon was audible again. Then suddenly they both were stunned by the glare of brilliant sunlight.

Momentarily blinded, Warren slammed on the brakes and

the car skidded to a stop. Then he leaned forward and simply stared, thunderstruck.

The road had vanished completely. The tall trees and the
steep slope had vanished, the overhanging rock on the other
side had also vanished.

They seemed perched on the very edge of a vast and
sunlit valley. The sky overhead was an eerie bluish-green,
with fluffy orange clouds dotted here and there.

There was a city down in that valley, a most unusual city.
They could distinctly see towers of large buildings, some of
bright glass and polished metal, others dull and strangely bul-
bous like a grotesque image of an Oriental metropolis. There
was the suggestion of a city wall and roadways leading
through it. There were banners flying from various towers—
and puffs of black smoke and evidence of objects hurtling
violently into the air as if from shocks of explosions.

Before this city stretched a broad, open field, and it was
occupied by what seemed to be two opposing armies facing
each other. Lines of men were charging, dust and smoke
arose, where men were locked in combat. Puffs of smoke
and flame showed where a bombardment was taking place.

They could not see these figures clearly; in fact they had
only an instant's glance at them, for something more immediate focused their attention.

They noticed now that a wide road ran up the rim of the
valley almost directly to their car. Coming up that road,
rolling toward them, came a column of armored machines.
They were big clumsy cars, rolling on numerous wheels instead of tractors. Exhaust pipes puffed steam from low on
their sides, and men in metal helmets perched on their sides
and tops.

The men in the first vehicles, which roughly resembled
outsized military tanks, spotted their car. Warren and Marge
saw them point and open their mouths to call out. The nearest steamer tank swung its guns on the car, the helmeted

crew leveling their weapons and craning their necks forward to get a good look at the two.

Marge's first instinct had been good. She raised her camera almost by reflex action and snapped the scene. Then she took her eye off the finder, looked at the tank charging at them, its gun now coming down to aim point-blank at them, and she screamed.

Her scream released Warren from the paralysis of astonishment which had gripped him. He popped his foot off the brake, stepped on the gas, and for an instant closed his eyes.

The road ahead was straight for a small stretch, he recalled. He opened his eyes again ready for the turn as he felt the car lurch forward.

There was no valley, no orange clouds, no exotic city, no tanks and soldiers. There was only the turn of the road coming at them fast; the trees and the rock. He swerved, went around it, and began to slow down, his forehead beaded with sweat, his body trembling from the reaction.

"*Ohhh!*" gasped Marge, letting her breath out with a sigh. She slumped back. And then they both heard it.

Mixed with the wild horn-signal behind them, came a shriek of brakes, a skidding sound, then a crashing and smashing from around the last bend.

"I guess our friend behind us missed the turn," said Warren, bringing the car almost to a halt. "Or he turned the wrong way—if and when he saw the vision."

"You going back?" asked Marge, turning to look behind. "I can't see a thing."

Warren stepped up his speed again. "This road is too narrow to turn around, and we might get mixed up with that mirage again. We'll keep on going. If we find anyone up ahead, we can send them back to rescue their man. We're still on this story, remember, and we're going to get it!"

"Then, for Pete's sake, drive slower!" the girl said. "Or all we'll get is an obit in *People*."

Warren grinned his approval at her. "Maybe you're right, at that," he conceded, and continued at a more reasonable pace. "But we did see a vision for ourselves, do you realize that?" he said. "And another thing: do you recall hearing any sounds from it? I *saw* bombs exploding, tanks moving, and men open their mouths and act as if they were yelling, but I didn't hear one doggone thing. Just the wind in the trees and the car. Did you hear anything from the vision?"

"Now that you mention it, no," she said. "But I did get a shot of it with my little thirty-five milli."

"But if all this is hallucination, your film will show just about what we see now," he said.

They drove on around another sharp, wooded turn, then found themselves on a level stretch, with the road widening rapidly. In a few more minutes the trees thinned out and they approached a building that resembled a Swiss chalet at the right side of the road. It was built of stucco and field stone, with dark brown timbers and ornately scrolled wood trim along the eaves of the sharply slanted roof.

Behind it, they made out portions of other buildings, half hidden by the foliage. These structures apparently had been built more recently than the chalet; they were of unadorned concrete; perfectly plain boxlike or oblong buildings. One of them, surprisingly enough, was simply a huge dome, made of some kind of metal, reminding Warren of the dome of a planetarium. The whole structure was windowless.

Warren pulled the car up before the door of the chalet. "I guess this is it," he said. "I'm going in. Coming?"

"You're not leaving me behind," she said, following him out of the car. They walked up to the door of the lodge. As they came to it, it opened.

Two men stood in the doorway. They were both big, husky men, with crew cuts. One of them, who had piercing blue eyes and a scar on his chin, looked at them with raised eyebrows.

"What're you doing here?" he said. "Who you wanna see?"

The other man, who had a flattened nose like a prize fighter, nudged the first man with his elbow. "Better have 'em come in, Jack. Better let the chief talk to 'em."

Jack nodded. He stood aside slightly, pointed inside with his thumb. "Come on in, folks."

Warren, about to identify himself to them, thought better of it. He'd rather see their employer. He grasped Marge's arm, grinned and whispered to her, "Step into my parlor, said the spider. . . ."

They found themselves in the dim anteroom of the chalet, and Flat-Nose closed the door quietly behind them.

CHAPTER FOUR

THEY WENT through the small antechamber and out into a large high-ceilinged room which appeared to occupy most of the ground floor. A huge stone fireplace occupied one wall; and there were many wide armchairs, a long plank trestle table, several bookcases, a large record player and a sizable collection of records in an open-faced cabinet. Doors led apparently to other parts of the house.

Marge and Warren stood for a minute under the silent inspection of Flat-Nose, while Jack went through one of the doors. In a minute he came back accompanied by an elderly gray-haired man conservatively dressed.

"Ah," said this individual, peering at them from sharp blue eyes beneath beetling gray brows. "And may I ask to what we owe this unexpected visit?"

Warren reached into his pocket, took out his wallet and extracted his press card. "Let me introduce myself and the young lady. We're from *People*. . . ."

The elderly man furrowed his brows and let Warren continue with the introduction. Then he nodded briefly. "My name is Enderby, Dr. James Enderby. I must inform you at once that your arrival here is most unfortunate. We are not at all desirous of publicity, and I must insist that you will find no story for your magazine here."

"Well," said Warren, still smiling, "perhaps not. But you may be able to shed some light on another story Miss McElroy and I have been working on. All our leads seemed to point up to Thunderhook Mountain—and you seem to be the ones occupying it."

"That's perfectly true," added Marge, who had seated herself in an armchair and was busily repairing her complexion with powder and lipstick. "You certainly seem awfully secretive. And inhospitable! I never saw such people! After the scare we had on the road, we have to meet a crew like you."

Enderby frowned sharply. "What 'scare' are you talking about, young lady?" Jack and Flat-Nose also wheeled around to stare at her.

Marge put down her compact and looked at Dr. Enderby with widened eyes. "Why, that drive-in movie show you gave on the road up here. It almost scared us to death! It wasn't funny."

"A—a drive-in movie show?" puzzled their host. "What are you talking about? What did you see?"

"Oh, come off it," Marge said. "I don't know how you've been managing these projections or whatever they are around the country, but I'm sure you know all about it, Doctor."

"What? Wha—" spluttered Enderby, confused and puzzled. But just as he was about to go on with whatever he was going to say, the front door of the chalet banged open, and a strange appearing figure burst into the large room.

It was their pursuer, but his jacket was in shreds, there were scratches on his face and hands, his pants were ripped and a smear of dirt ran all along the side of his chest and on his cheek. He was clearly fit to be tied.

When this newcomer saw Warren and Marge, he gave a yell. "There they are!" he shouted. "If it wasn't for them, and their damn' snooping . . ."

Jack and Flat-Nose grabbed him by the elbows. "Hey, take it easy, Kenster. Sit down. What happened? Did you run off the road?"

Kenster slumped into a chair, still staring angrily at the two intruders. "What do you think? I was chasing these two, trying to get them to come back and get off this road. They got no business up here. And . . ."

He hesitated, clearly unwilling to speak of the vision on the mountain side. Warren took the opportunity to help him out. "You ran into that mirage, saw the men with the tanks, and lost control, eh?"

Kenster rubbed a scratch on his cheek. "I lost the road when that happened. Went over into the slope. The car's jammed among the trees, thirty feet down the side. Shoulda been you."

"Now wait," said Enderby, breaking in. "You, Kenster, get to your quarters and fix yourself up. Get those scratches taken care of and change your clothes. We'll take care of the car later."

As Kenster slouched out and could be heard stomping upstairs, Warren turned sharply on Enderby.

"Now, look here," he said. "There's something very strange going on here and it's my job to get to the bottom of it. People are seeing disturbing visions all around this district

and quite evidently you're in a position to shed some light
on it. You hide yourself away here up on a mountain, have
guards to keep people from checking up on you. Why, you
act like a collection of criminals or conspirators!

"This young lady and I are members of the staff of an
important national magazine. You can't hold us prisoners
without that becoming known to our publisher and subse-
quently to the newspapers. You can't conceal what's going
on here and expect us to co-operate with your schemes. I
think you had better make clear who you are and what this
establishment represents, without further nonsense."

Enderby stared at him thoughtfully. "I'm not intimidated
by you or your position. I think I could quash any publicity
you may try to foist on us. It happens that there is nothing
criminal going on here. These buildings and this entire mountain top, for hundreds of acres, is the property of the Lansing
Foundation. We who work here are employees of that
Foundation, and we are engaged on certain researches of a
highly confidential nature. I must advise you that this work
is being carried on with the full knowledge and sanction of
the United States Government, and if necessary I would not
hesitate to call in the authorities to prevent any knowledge
of our activities getting in the public press."

Warren was startled. The Lansing Foundation was one
of the wealthiest research organizations in the country. Set
up on the death of Walter Lansing, founder and president of
the huge Lansing automobile firm, it diverted a substantial
share of its wealth into a non-profit foundation "for the
advancement of knowledge." He knew that the Lansing Foundation had endowed many technical colleges throughout the
world, that it had uderwritten several valuable scientific
projects, that it was credited with many achievements that
had markedly benefitted science and invention. The Lansing
Foundation was not a name to be taken lightly. It was indeed
possible that its work would be protected by the government

for security reasons, if the work veered in such a direction.

Nevertheless Warren continued his efforts. "The Lansing Foundation, Doctor, is not the government. And when the work of one of its branches is such as to interfere with the peace and safety of innocent citizens, such as those in Coningo County, it is the duty of the press to explain it, and if necessary, to combat it. It is quite clear that some operation up here is creating all sorts of frightening mirages, visions, and scares—setting up the groundwork that might lead to national panic. *People* will not be intimidated by your foundation's money and size. I might point out that we are not without public influence ourselves."

Enderby pursed his lips, began to get a little angry. But before he could answer Warren, he was interrupted.

From a rear door in the huge room, a man bustled through. This newcomer was wearing a white smock and was carrying several papers in his hand. He glanced up, saw Enderby and started rapidly towards him.

"Yes, Dr. Weidekind?" said Enderby, annoyed at the interruption.

Weidekind, a tall, thin man with pale washed-out blue eyes and a shock of straw-colored hair, seemed not to notice anyone else. "We had a little phasing trouble with the restrainers, Jim," he said to Enderby, speaking rapidly. "There may have been another sympathetic mirage somewhere. Especially in connection with our viewers. We had a full-charted phase of the Steam Eon of Planet Two of NNW Two Sixty-five. A fine war struggle. I think we'll have to increase the power of radial bank East."

"All right, Weidekind, I suspected as much. Don't discuss it here, we have visitors," Enderby said quickly the moment he managed to break into Weidekind's rush of words.

For the first time the pale-eyed scientist seemed to notice the others. "Oh," he said, then glanced at Enderby. The latter quickly added, "Go back and shut down the restrainers. I'll be back as soon as I can get away."

Weidekind nodded, stared at Marge curiously, and hurried off. There was a hush in the room for a moment, as each one tried to readjust to the astonishing interruption.

Warren became aware of something that he had noticed subconsciously all along. There had been a high-pitched distant humming somewhere in the rear of the building since they had first come in the door. This had been present, and yet so steady that it had not penetrated his mind. Now he listened to it—in fact, he noticed that all the others seemed straining to hear it too at the same time. Then suddenly it changed pitch. It dropped to a lower hum, as if someone had turned a control or turned off some minor generator.

Warren was also considering Weidekind's strange remarks, and now he broke the brief silence. "If you are engaged in communication with other planets, it might be wise for you to co-operate with the press. This is a very big story; you cannot hope to conceal it long."

Enderby looked at him for a moment, puzzled. "Communicating with other planets? Why. . . ." He let his voice trail off.

At this moment the guard Kenster returned to the room, a little cleaner, but still angry. "I got an idea, Chief," he said. "It would solve everything. Why don't you let me take these two pests, just drive them down the mountain and dump them and their car over the cliff. That way they get killed the way they almost got me killed; and we keep our secret and everything is okay again. Huh?"

"Yeah," put in Flat-Nose. "That's a good idea. Why not let us get it over with for you?"

Jack, the third guard, looked angry. He was a big husky man, as were the others, but evidently of a slightly less sanguinary nature. "Aw, don't listen to them," he said. "We can't do that. Especially with this neat chick here." He glanced at Marge appreciatively.

Marge looked at him. "Thanks, You've got some rough playmates."

But Warren didn't think it funny. Kenster and Flat-Nose actually had meant what they had said. Hastily he warned Enderby that if such a thing were to be tried, they could be sure it would be found out. Especially with as big a publisher as C. B. Carlyle behind them.

Enderby had seemed as shocked at the suggestion as the two reporters but he still appeared to be trying to find a way out. "Did you say C. B. Carlyle?" he asked.

Warren nodded. Enderby asked him about Carlyle's relationship to their project and seemed interested in learning that it had been the publisher personally who had sent Warren Alton after the story.

"Let me make a call to the Foundation headquarters in New York," said Enderby at last. "I think they may be able to straighten this out."

He went over to a desk at a far side of the room, and picked up the phone.

For a while there was silence. The guards drew off by themselves and talked in whispers, glancing every so often at the intruders. Warren took a notebook and pencil from his pocket and started hastily writing in it.

The door at the far end, from where the mysterious humming noise came, opened and several men came in, doffing white smocks. Weidekind was one of them. As they entered the general room, they had the appearance of men about to relax after a busy day.

Two dropped into easy chairs and glanced through newspapers and magazines. Weidekind came over to Warren, while another went to the record player and started hunting through the racked discs.

"I'm sorry I interrupted you," Weideikind said apologetically. "I wasn't aware you had business with the chief."

"That's all right," replied Warren. "It wasn't exactly business. . . . And I suppose your work came first." He went on to introduce himself and Marge.

Hans Weideiknd bowed slightly in acknowledgment. "Charmed," he said. "It isn't often we have the pleasure of a pretty young lady at our retreat up here. The only members of the fair sex around are rather oldish and stout."

Marge laughed. "Goodness!" she said. "Don't you ever get to town? Too busy watching the doings of our Martian friends?"

Weideikind raised his eyebrows. "Well, Martians isn't precisely the right word. However—" A dark-haired man in his thirties interrupted the scientist. "Introduce us, Hans," this one said.

The newcomer's name was Louis Marco. The man who had been about to start the record player until Enderby's signal at the telephone had halted him, turned out to be Roger Stanhope. The others now in the room were Leopold Steiner, balding and fortyish, wearing thick spectacles, and Carter Williams, younger, with light brown curly hair and a Middle-Western accent.

"You men look like engineers to me," said Warren. "Am I right, or are you just instructors in experimental farming?"

There was a general laugh. "We're not from State Agricultural, that's for sure," said Stanhope. "No, I guess we're engineers of a sort. Surprised you didn't hear of Steiner and Marco here, though. I thought you were up on things at *People*. Didn't you see the write-ups they got in your competitors' science departments a year ago?"

Warren thought back. He'd probably been away on some foreign assignment. But Marge said unexpectedly, "I think I noticed your pictures in *People*, too. I checked through the files a week ago. You had some theories about galaxies or something?"

Steiner beamed, but Warren carried the ball. "I thought you were astrophysicists. Is this an observatory, then?"

Before anyone could answer, Enderby hung up the phone and walked over to the group. "Be careful what you say, gentlemen, please. Mr. Alton, I believe you say your publisher is C. B. Carlyle?"

At Warren's nod, Enderby continued: "Will you please go over and telephone Mr. Carlyle from here? He will have instructions for you."

The reporter was surprised. He walked over to the desk, sat down, and picked up the phone. When he got the office operator, he gave her the number of Carlyle's direct wire. After a little wait, he heard his publisher's voice.

"Hello, Alton?" said Carlyle. "I see you got to the root of the story. Good work. However, I'm changing your instructions. It seems that the Lansing Foundation has a story several times bigger than the atom bomb. I don't know exactly what it is, but I've arranged with the directors at Lansing headquarters here to let you and your photographer stay on up there until they've completed their experiment. In exchange for our press silence until their job is finished, they'll allow you and Miss McElroy to become their official chroniclers. You two will remain on Thunderhook and help out. You are to write the popular version of their official report when it's done. Miss McElroy will help take the official pictures of the work as it's being done.

"How long? I gather from Jim Enderby—he won the Nobel Prize in physics seven years ago, remember?—that their work may have several months to go. Stick with it. It may be the biggest story of our lifetime. Give them a hand if they want you to—I understand they can use some help.

"Do I know what it is about? No, but I trust Jim Enderby. You'll know soon enough. I'll see that your pay checks are mailed to you regularly. Only thing I know about it is the name—Project Microcosm. Whatever that means—but it'll be an exclusive under your by-line for *People*, if and when. Okay? Put Enderby on and I'll confirm it."

Warren handed the receiver to Enderby, stood up and walked slowly back, aware of the questioning eyes of Marge and the scientists on him. Project Microcosm? Now what could that signify?

CHAPTER FIVE

"Well, Dr. Enderby," Warren said, "it appears that you've acquired two new members of your staff, according to C. B. Carlyle. I hope you can put us up without inconveniencing anyone?"

Dr. Enderby nodded, reached out his hand, and Warren shook it solemnly. "Good. We can use you, as a matter of fact. We are really horribly understaffed."

Marge stood up and looked around. "I hope I'm not the only girl in the party."

Enderby laughed. "Oh no, Miss McElroy. We have at least two ladies on our staff—our capable cook and our housekeeper. So you'll not be entirely on your own. . . . Now, I believe it's time for lunch."

As he said the last, a large, cheerful appearing middle-aged woman, came in and began setting a long table before the fireplace. Apparently she was the cook. A thin, aging man assisted her. In a short while all the company, including the three guards, were seated and enjoying lunch. Nobody made any reference to the nature of their work, and the conversation was light and casual. Warren noted with amusement that already Marge was the target of Jack's and Kenster's eyes. She would have no trouble adjusting.

As they were drinking coffee, he broached the subject. What, he wanted to know, was Project Microcosm.

As Enderby paused to form an answer, Kenster spoke up. "I think it's a mistake to allow them in on this. They haven't been passed by security and we aren't supposed to take any chances. I think you are forgetting that this work would be of extreme value to foreign spies. We absolutely should take no chances, none at all. How do we know for sure these people are what they claim?"

Louis Marco nodded. "With all due respect, I think we ought to consider that carefully. There are some things of very grave consequence here . . ."

Enderby waved a hand impatiently. "I grant the danger, but let me say that I have faith in the Lansing directors and also in Mr. Carlyle, the publisher. And let me say further that it is at present far better for us to keep an eye on our new additions rather than to let them go, or let them be lodged in jail."

Warren had been taking this in with some trepidation. Before there were further objections to Enderby's stand, Warren rose and said, "If we are going to be initiated, perhaps you would have the time to show us the layout. We still don't know what is going on here."

Enderby nodded. "Yes, I was planning on taking you around." He turned to the others. "Who is on duty at the observatory now?"

Steiner said, "Rendell. I'm going to relieve him shortly."

Enderby rose, and Warren and Marge with him. They followed him out the side door and found themselves on the grounds facing the series of concrete structures behind the main lodge. As they walked Enderby outlined the project.

"You will find much of what is doing here very unusual. Inside that hemispherical dome is probably the strangest sight in all of man's existence—and yet it is entirely man-made. I wonder if you remember Dr. Steiner's work at all? It made some scientific headlines a few years ago."

Warren nodded. "I was wondering why his name seemed familiar. It seems to me that he was prominent in the atomic energy laboratories at Hanford, and then later advanced some unique theories regarding atomic forces. Hadn't heard anything about him lately."

"Yes, that's the man. In a sense Project Microcosm is Steiner's own concept. He presented it to the Lansing Foundation, and we took it up."

As they talked they arrived at a squat cement building. "This houses our atomic pile. It was a necessary adjunct to supply the kind of power we needed to work our project. Don't try to go inside without letting them know. It's well shielded, but you shouldn't take chances."

Behind the building housing the pile were three long buildings; one the dormitory, one a place where files and records were kept, another housing calculating machines and special research rooms. They did not go into these buildings, but simply had them pointed out. As they walked Enderby seemed to be taking them around the hemispherical dome, as if to keep that until the last.

As they arrived finally before its door, Enderby stopped. "Inside here is Project Microcosm itself. It is, as you will see, just what its name implies."

They went in. Inside they found themselves on a balcony that circled the interior of the dome. It seemed larger viewed from within than from the outside. For inside it was a true sphere, the latter half extending into the ground as deep as the top half was raised above the ground. The balcony circled the inside of the shell.

They looked over the rail. And for minutes Marge and

Warren simply stared, their minds numb with amazement.

They were looking into what seemed the sky itself. They looked down and outward and what they saw was a sphere of dense black dotted with brilliantly gleaming points of intense light. They saw a slow swirl of seeming white dust forming a long curving pattern that dissected the main half of the black mass, cutting through the center.

The black mass was not solid; rather it gave the impression of being utterly empty, and yet sprinkled with a myriad infinitesimal sparks, shining and cutting through it. There was the effect of motion, as if each spark was moving and as if the central spiral misty mass was slowly in revolution, each glittering facet of it alive and fighting against the eye-paining blackness—which was not so much blackness as a simple lack of existence there.

Looking into it they had the impression of looking down into infinite depths, of being about to fall outwards into unending space. The glittering points of light hurt their eyes and tantalized them at the same time. They wanted to look away and they were afraid that if they did they would miss something wonderful.

After a few minutes Warren wrenched his eyes away, looked forcibly at Enderby standing next to him watching him with a half smile. He shook his head to clear it. "My God!" the reporter said. "What is it? It's marvelous—and it's frightening."

Marge looked up. She was pale and stunned. "It's like looking into the skies," she murmured. "It's like something you dream about when you're a child."

Enderby smiled. "It is like looking into the skies, because it *is* a sky. It's the microcosm, a real miniature universe. The bright lights are stars; yes, real stars on an infinitesimal scale, and the black is the depths of space of another universe."

"Another universe?" muttered Warren, looking again.

"Yes, it's unmistakable. What a marvelous projection! What a fantastic planetarium!"

"No," said Enderby, "it's not a projection and not a planetarium. It's real. It's what it seems to be. It's a true universe."

Warren looked up again. "How can that be? A universe in a dome . . . ? No; it's delusion or illusion."

"No delusion," said the voice of Steiner, who had quietly joined them. "No delusion. Come over to the telescopes here and look for yourself."

Warren and Marge turned. Now they noticed that around the balcony at various points were grouped instruments—telescopes, spectroscopes, and many instruments whose uses were not at once apparent. As Steiner walked over to the nearest telescope, they followed him. At once they experienced a curious sensation. Walking in the vicinity of the microcosm was eerie. There was a feeling as if forces were dragging at them, as if invisible waves were flowing around them.

Warren wavered, and Enderby gasped. "Oh, I should have warned you. If you've a watch on you, it's ruined now. I simply forgot. Here at the project we never carry instruments like that on us. There are very powerful magnetic forces encircling this experiment; they are the means we use to control it."

They reached the telescope—a large refractor mounted on gimbals along the railing. Steiner glanced into it, stood aside. "Look into it, Mr. Alton. Look at anything. You will see. It's real."

Warren put his eye to the lens, adjusted the vision. He saw a field of black sky with stars sprinkled through it. But the stars were not twinkling and soft as seen through an astronomical telescope. They were hard and bright. He turned the dials and as he did so the view shifted steadily. Suddenly a bright object sprang into view. It was a star, closeup—and he could see the brilliant disc of flaming white and the flaring arms of the star's flaming corona as it hurled mighty columns of gas far from its surface.

He stared transfixed, until Marge nudged him and he reluctantly surrendered the telescope to her. "It looks like a star," said the reporter at last. "But it must be so tiny. How could it continue like that without burning out?"

Steiner shook his head. "It is not tiny, not at all. That star is, within its own universe, as large as our sun, probably larger. Those gas clouds, its corona, are thousands of miles high."

Warren stared at him. "Impossible. You are contradicting yourself. First you say it is not a projection or delusion, and is here. Then you say it is millions of times larger than this whole room—or maybe our whole world. It cannot be both."

"It cannot, and yet it is," said Steiner firmly. "This is a genuine universe we have here. It occupies a space of its own. It is not part of our own space. Within its own being, its size is as great as that of our entire galaxy; it stretches many hundreds of light years, yet to us, who are *outside* its space-time continuum, it seems small.

"But notice this. We cannot penetrate it. Watch." He took a pole from a niche in the wall, held it out, tried to poke it into the black pulsing sphere of the microcosm. It touched or seemed to touch the outside and stopped. "Here, take the pole, push," he shoved the end of it into Warren's hand.

Warren took it, pushed. It was like pushing against a wall of steel. So far could the pole go, but the instant it touched the outermost edge of the micro-universe it stopped. Warren thrust with all his strength but it was ineffective.

"It would take more power to push that pole one-millionth of an inch into the microcosm than there is available in the entire world," said Steiner softly. "For the thing you see there is not in this universe at all."

Marge took her eye away from the scope. "I see it, so

there's something there. It's got to be here, on earth. Who are you kidding?"

Steiner waved them to a low bench set along the inner wall of the building. "Sit down; I'll tell you how it came to be, and why it is what it is."

They walked back and sat down. Their eyes were fixed on the weird sight of the pulsing micro-universe. Steiner himself, who should have been so familiar with it, also kept his eyes on it. It was so awe-inspiring that, whatever it was, no one could look away from it for long.

"This all came out of an idea I had about ten years ago," began Dr. Steiner. "While I don't expect that you are too well acquainted with modern physics outside of what you have read in popularizations, you probably do know that as a result of our atomic energy studies we have been making tremendous advances in our knowledge of the structure of matter and of the universe."

"Of course," nodded Alton.

"Much of this was due to the invention and perfection of the cyclotron, a device which enables us to observe particles of matter at hitherto inconceivable speed and thus to bring out properties not suspected before. The cyclotron has undergone vast changes, the present bevatron, for instance, is capable of immense operations.

"Due to our research in the splitting of atoms and the analysis of the particles so liberated, we have found that matter and energy can be found in far more forms than was previously supposed. We have classified dozens of different types of sub-atomic particles now, and among them certain ones like the anti-proton and the anti-neutron which clearly did not appear to exist normally in our own universe. These particles have the same properties as the normal particles of our own matter, yet because their electrical charge is exactly reversed, they could not exist in contact with any part of our universe for more than a fraction of a second. And yet we found that nature permitted such things to be conceived—yes, even permitted the concept of anti-matter, whole structures, molecules, masses, all similar in every way to the normal matter and molecules of our universe—and yet absolutely unable to exist in context with our universe. The idea of this mirror-image matter was possible, yet nowhere could we hope to find it. But we could, strange to say, *make* it. Keep it in existence, no; but make it, yes.

"And that was one angle of my idea," Steiner stopped, glanced at them to see if they had followed him.

"This is an anti-matter universe?" asked Warren pointing at the microcosm.

"Frankly I don't know," said Steiner. "Probably not. But the idea arose out of this thought. The thought was that we could create that which did not exist in this universe and that which physically *was not allowed* to exist in this universe —and yet which could be created. That was one staggering thought.

"The next was an idea which arose from a conjunction of two laws of physics. The first has to do with the changes in the mass of a particle as it approaches the speed of light. Einstein, followed by the work of Lorenz and Fitzgerald, determined that a moving object gained mass and lengthened in the direction of infinity as it approached the speed of light. Theoretically at the very speed of light a particle would be of infinite mass and infinite length.

"In our work at the cyclotrons, we determined that this was indeed so. Definite measurements of particles that had been raced up to close to that speed showed a strong and rapidly rising increase in their mass—so much so that it seemed as if it would always be impossible to supply enough energy to bring the particle finally to that ultimate speed." He paused to take breath. The two listeners did not interrupt him.

"The other factor which occurred to me was at first irrelevant. This is almost the opposite end of the research spectrum. The idea of absolute zero in temperature. It is known that the temperature of an object is the product of the relative speed of its molecules. As a body heats up, its molecules are farther apart from each other and move faster. As it loses heat, they slow down and approach each other. At absolute zero, the molecules would lose all motion, come to a dead stop. Such a stop would presumably cause all the molecules to come together, to form one mass without internal motion. This, too, seemed an unattainable vista. Experiments had produced temperatures of only fractions above absolute, but again the final zero could not be attained.

"It was my idea to combine both operations. To attempt to have a particle of matter reach both the speed of light and absolute zero simultaneously. I had a hunch—one of those queer inspirations that come out of nothing sometimes when you are working on a difficult problem—that by combining the cyclotronic speed-up with ultra-refrigeration methods—I might solve both. The addition of mass to a particle brought near absolute zero might be the extra factor. And vice versa.

"For you see, there is this about the speed of light and the absolute zero of temperature—both are apparently boundaries of our universe. Both are part of the restraining walls of our very cosmos."

Steiner paused lost in thought. Warren looked at the pulsing stars flickering in the impenetrable depths of the microcosm. He waited silently.

"I proposed this idea and worked at it for four years before I finally saw how it could be done. At the same time Marco and Weidekind were working out the mathematical probabilities of the results. When we compared notes we saw what was coming. We took our work to the Lansing Foundation, explained it, and they granted us the means to continue our experiment, to put it into operation. They realized that the outcome might be inconceivably wonderful. They were right."

"What happened?" said Marge in an awed voice.

"The result of the experiment, the achievement of bringing a particle of matter to infinite mass and infinite length at absolute zero was the creation of a *thing* which could not exist in our universe. Obviously our universe cannot contain something of infinite mass and length, nor could a particle of the absolute solidity of absolute zero remain fixed. What happened was that the germ of a new universe was created. What happened, in short, was the creation by artificial means of exactly the same kind of super-primal atom as must have existed at the very origin of creation. An atom of hydrogen, infinite in mass, occupying all space, and packed to a density that encompassed in itself the whole potential of a universe of matter.

"This was the same type of particle that astro-physicists now believe existed at the dawn of our own universe, four and a half billion years ago!"

Steiner stopped, ran a hand through his sparse hair. "Such a primordial super-atom could be created. And when it was created, it must and would tear itself out of our own universe and make for itself another universe; it would create a space-time continuum of its own; one having no relation, dependence on, or connection with our own.

"The result of these calculations at first seemed self-defeating. It meant apparently that at the moment of our triumph, the primordial hydrogen atom would simply cease to exist as far as we were concerned. But later calculations showed that by surrounding the experiment with certain magnetic forces, by conducting it under certain stresses, it would not vanish but would encapsule itself—would simply form for itself a bubble in our own cosmos and would contain itself therein.

"We succeeded in producing this primordial universe-atom

here on Thunderhook four years ago. You see it before you now."

Warren answered slowly, "But that which is before us is no atom. That's a miniature galactic system."

Steiner said, "Yes. This is the primordial hydrogen atom as it appears some billions of its years later. The atom could not remain stable. It exploded—just as did the primordial universe-atom which was once the whole of our own universe. And it is not miniature—it is as large as our whole Milky Way galaxy."

"You've lost me," Marge said. "It isn't even as big as this building. Who are you trying to kid?"

CHAPTER SIX

STEINER laughed a little. "I know it seems hard to believe; the evidence of our eyes is so persuasive. Let me change my remark. In itself and to itself it is as large as our own galaxy. It is about a hundred thousand light years in diameter. We know this is so, for that is the true measurement of the speed of light *within* this microcosm. *Its* light, which travels at the same speed as our own light and has the same properties, would take a ray one hundred thousand revolutions of one of its Earth-type planets around its primary sun to cross from one edge of this micro-universe to the other.

"So you are right in one way; to us, and judged only by our relative standards, this is a small object. But it does not obey the laws of this universe; it obeys only those laws of nature which adjust to its magnitude in the same fashion as its internal light. Since we ourselves cannot physically penetrate into this universe, then we must judge it only by its own standards.

"You see, it is a true independent space-time unit. In the last four of our years, it has passed through a billion of its years—and its internal particles have passed through a similar period of evolutionary development. You will see this for yourself later when you study our records and photos. From an exploding super-atom of hydrogen it has today reached a point where it has the same elements of our own universe, where it has suns of many types and ages, where these suns have planetary attendants, where they are grouped together roughly in a spiral disc galaxy."

Marge still shook her head. "I still say it's small."

Warren turned to her. "I think what he means is that if you were in there—a person on one of its worlds and the same size to that world as you are to the Earth—why it would be a universe in size."

"Well," said the girl slowly, "I can get that all right. But what does it prove?"

"Yes," added Warren. "What do you hope to learn from it? After all, I seem to remember from my college astronomy that our own universe contains not just one but hundreds and probably thousands of galaxies—and that it is constantly expanding and apparently infinite. This microcosm of yours is obviously smaller than ours, contains but one galaxy and plainly can't expand much more, and certainly it isn't infinite."

Steiner nodded. "Quite right, but you overlook the value of this. In the first place—and this was our original thought —it served as the experimental proof of theories regarding the creation of our own universe. By watching it develop we are able to trace the evolution of our own system of stars, to watch the birth of planets, to test the actual working out of cosmic forces far too vast and slow in our own universe for us to grasp.

"We have gathered masses of absolutely invaluable data on the forces that went into the creation of our sun and our planet and our human species. What is even more important is that we shall also see the working out of the end of a galaxy. We shall see what will happen when our own system grows old, when our own sun cools, and when our own galaxy comes eventually to old age and to some sort of cosmic death. What this will be is still only hypothesis. But in the next few months here at Thunderhook we will have the answers.

"This little microcosm is limited, and yet because its natural laws are essentially the same as ours, what it will do as it dies out will accurately mirror the end of our own galaxy. Not of our universe, it is true, for ours is, as you say, infinite and expanding. We have blocked the expansion of this one with our magnetic interference, and thus have established a barrier through which this micro-universe cannot penetrate. So it has but the one galaxy and is strictly finite.

"As a result of this limitation, it has gone through in one billion of its years what has taken us four and a half billion of our years."

Warren looked again at the pulsing everchanging marvel. "If what you say is so, then it must have planets that are at the level of Earth—and these planets may have life on them. Perhaps one or two even have intelligent life."

"Yes," said Steiner, "yes, yes. And that is the most wonderful discovery we have made. We didn't predict it, but the results of that will be priceless. For there are planets of this microcosm that have life! Planets sufficiently like Earth in mass and atmosphere and warmth to have life—and we watched this life evolve! And on fifteen of these worlds that life is almost where Earth life is now—with human-like beings and growing civilizations. On many more there are other human-types coming up the road fast!

"Do you realize what this means? It means that when these micro-civilizations surpass us, go on to where we will be a thousand, ten thousand, maybe a million years from where we are, we will be able to use their super-inventions! In a few months more here at Thunderhook we may be in possession of the secret of perfected atomic-power machines, of anti-gravity devices, of perfected, advanced spaceships, of some kind of star-drive, if that is ever possible! We will know because we will watch them develop it in the millions of years they have still to go—*in their time!*

"And then we shall see how a world ends . . . this, too. But meanwhile these things make our project the world's most valuable. The secrets we shall find will benefit humanity immeasurably!"

Steiner was leaning over the railing as he went on, staring intensely into the black depths of the microcosm. He was as a man inspired. Marge was impressed. Steiner got control of himself, sat down again, mopped his brow. "This thing astonishes me even now. Forgive me for getting excited."

"I don't blame you," said Warren. "You were getting to me, too."

"Yes," said Marge, "but look: If you can't get into this microcosm, how can you see all those inventions? If these worlds are moving so fast in relation to us, then you can't see what's going on. Maybe with a fast-action camera, but are your telescopes good enough to see the small things on the surfaces? If those are suns, how can you see the planets?"

"A good question," said Steiner. "Frankly it stumped us after a while. The experiment was all right before planets began to form from the cosmic gas clouds, but after that we were up against the same problem. We do have powerful telescopes and we can see the planets. But we were not able to detect the details of life on their surfaces until a strange phenomenon was detected. That was what we call sympathetic phase visions."

"Sounds like the mirages we've been chasing," said Warren.

Steiner nodded. "That's what they were. Because this is a universe of its own, its internal forces are vast and potent. They were able—as soon as some of its internal particles assumed a similar vibrational and physical phasing with our Earth itself—to set up sympathetic vibrations on our own world. We began to see visions around here several weeks ago here on Thunderhook a good deal, and I gather around the vicinity—occasionally to our embarrassment.

"Once a world within this microcosm sufficiently resembles Earth some part of it will, for reasons not quite determined, set up a sort of corresponding ring or vibration on some roughly similar bit of our own Earth. This takes the form of a mirage—a full dimensional vision of some scene which is in phase in the world of the micro-universe.

"Thus there was one wherein a section of a planet still in the primeval jungle period, with its beasts in the dinosaurian stage, was reflected or phased onto a farm near here."

"Bassett's farm!" gasped Marge.

"Yes," continued Steiner, "and many more things—flying beasts, sections of sky, bits of scenes, and now I hear from Weidekind an actual human scene; an event in some war going on on a world that is already very close to our level of civilization.

"These are very displeasing to us in one way—they call attention to our work. We have been trying out various means of blocking them, channeling them. We think that some additional magnetic blocks will cancel these mirages now.

"On the other hand, they afforded the first means of determining what was actually occurring on the planetary surfaces. There was a later side-effect even more fascinating.

This you will learn for yourself eventually. By this other method, we can know *all* that goes on—*really* all."

He fell silent. Warren and Marge got to their feet, walked slowly around the balcony looking into the microcosm from various angles. They saw that there were many telescopes set up. Most of these had photographic attachments constantly rolling, so that there was a steady record kept of everything occurring within the microcosm.

They returned to Steiner who was examining some spectrographic records. He looked up as they came to him again. "May I suggest now that you go to the record hall—I think Enderby must have shown it to you. Someone will be there who will be able to show you the photos of the various periods of our experiment. They are fascinating, I assure you."

Marge and Warren went out the way they had come in. Outside they stopped, looked up at the blue sky and the green grass and simultaneously took deep breaths. "Gosh," said Marge, "it felt strange in there. It felt somehow like playing God—and it scared me."

"I know what you mean," said Warren. "It was like being out of this world. It makes one feel as if one had been away on a distant trip and had just returned to the glorious sunlight of Earth. I think we are very lucky to witness this. You know this could be a turning point in the history of mankind."

Marge looked up at him a moment. "Warren, I think you're still a little woozy. I'm not sure I believe it."

"Suppose we go on to the records hall and look at the photos. That's more up your alley. Surely they will convince you. If they're fake, you should be able to tell."

"Yes," said the girl. "Come on."

The records hall was one of the long buildings that Enderby had pointed out before. They walked across the grass to it, found the door. It was locked. Warren knocked on it with his fist.

There was an interval, then they heard footsteps hurrying to the door, and it opened. "Oh, hullo," said Roger Stanhope, gazing out at them. He was wearing a white smock and holding a folder in his hands. "Come on in."

They entered and found themselves in a long room filled with filing cases, projectors and viewing screens. Beyond was a small door which opened on a developing laboratory. "I was inside sorting out some stuff," said Stanhope. "Really I'm getting quite annoyed. It seems to me that someone is constantly poking around in here without telling me. I'm supposed to be the chief photographer and records keeper here. And I wish they'd let me know."

They were all walking toward the end room as he talked, having locked the door behind them again. Warren remarked, "Has everyone got a key to this place?"

"Oh no," said Stanhope. "Goodness, no. Nobody but myself and Steiner and Marco and Enderby have keys. And I'm sure it wasn't them because they wouldn't be messing things up. Someone is getting in here and using my developers and tanks and mixing up my latest files. I wish they'd *ask* me."

They were in the developing room now. Reels of film were drying on racks, others were being prepared. A sheaf of folders was scattered over the broad work table. Warren looked at them. "Why would they come in without your permission?" he asked.

Stanhope waved his hands. "Heaven knows. Very annoying—and it's been going on for ever so long."

Marge whistled. "Maybe Kenster was right—maybe there is a spy here."

"Spies!" gasped Stanhope. "You mean a spy is coming in here and copying things? Why—I never thought of it!"

Warren looked around. "How often do you find things moved around or out of place?"

Stanhope pursed his lips. "Well, really not too often. I'd say it seems to happen about once a week, more or less. I really hadn't thought about it; just assumed one of the authorized three had been in. But lately it's been getting a bit irritating. You see we've been accumulating records at a great rate lately. Ever since they worked out the slow-down controls on the microcosm."

"Slow-down? What's that?" asked Warren, looking at some of the photos of star fields lying on the table.

"Oh," said Stanhope, "well, maybe you better start going through the general photo record. You'll understand the need for it better as you get on. Here, in this file here," he walked out of the developing room back to the mail records hall and pulled open a file drawer, "you'll find a general survey of our work. It was arranged as a simple historical sequence for publication eventually, after we take the wraps off the project.

"Take seats at the bench there and spread the pictures out as you go. You'll find descriptions of each sequence attached, but I hope the pictures will speak for themselves."

Warren and the girl sat down as directed and Warren started through the fat file of photos. He followed them in sequence and read aloud from the accompanying descriptive captions. Within minutes the two found themselves enthralled as there unrolled the whole history of a universe—a history that paralleled the birth pangs of our own cosmos, and revealed secrets of nature which no man had ever dreamed could be unfolded before.

The first pictures showed simply the setting up of the Thunderhook layout, the activation of the powerful atomic pile which supplied the vast energies needed, the setting up of the initial experiment.

Then followed a single photo showing a brilliant white ball, alone in blackness. This was the primordial atom as it had first materialized. It was featureless, white, and around it was a thin shell of black. Outside the black shell could be seen the edges of the instruments of the laboratory.

"This was taken in the first microsecond of the experiment. But look at what happened in the very next microsecond!"

The next photo showed that the globe had already started to expand. In a matter of microseconds, the primordial single compact massive atom of hydrogen had already exploded, was pushing outwards at a seemingly vast rate, extending steadily. As it extended the black border of the space envelope surrounding it expanded. The elements of the original atom seemed to fill all the area of the encapsuled space-time segment. Soon the photos showed a universal grayness as the elementary sub-electronic dust of the original explosion filled all the area of the universe. Then, hours later evidently, this began to thin out, patches of black appeared, and it could be seen that the dust was coagulating to form clouds and other areas where no dust seemed left. Now the pictures showed an area filled with misty nebulae—the unformed stuff of which stars are made.

Section by section the two watched the universe take shape. In the first half year of the Project work, they saw the first stars begin to take form, they saw the main gas cloud assume its spiral disc shape, and saw that the little cloudlets of gas, the nebulae, were also mainly discoid in shape. Special shots taken of certain of these showed that within the gassy discs there were bright spots and darker spots. A point of atomic explosion was accumulating at the center and radiating around it were specks of dark where non-explosive matter was forming and jelling. They followed one of these sequences to a point where after the first year they saw a solar system formed—a glowing star and six tiny planets revolving around it.

"And this, says the comment, represented the first third of a billion relative years of this micro-universe. Three hundred millions years compressed into one of our years!" exclaimed Warren.

They shuffled through a number of planetary formations,

saw that the general configuration of the microcosm now
had taken much the form of the micro-universe as they saw
it. Stars were recognizable, and the spiral shape of its one
galaxy was beginning to be recognizable. Many nebulous
clouds still remained, and these were to thin out during the
next seven hundred million—relative—years.

They followed sequences of the formation of planets.
They saw systems with two planets and systems with as many
as fifteen. Now greater magnification began to bring them
close-ups of star surfaces in blazing coronal glory, and of
planets. They saw the planets as molten masses, glowing and
red. They saw them covered with great clouds of steam and
gases. They saw some lose their atmospheric envelopes and
become sterile rocky masses. They saw others become great
gaseous globes of belted atmosphere rings, like such worlds
as Jupiter and Uranus. And they saw some that began to
shape up like Earth-type worlds, worlds with land and sea
areas, poles and clear atmospheres.

On some of these they saw some amazing photography,
microsecond work, of rough surfaces, of great deserts, of
clefts and volcanic action, of rows of mighty volcanoes, and
of huge cloudbanks shot through with lightning.

And as they watched the second year of the Thunderhook
work they saw that the micro-universe planets were settling
down, assuming sufficient surface peace to allow for the
development of life. They saw how green covered the land
as fern forests climbed out of the ocean depths, and they
saw tantalizing shots that indicated animal life—very tantalizing, for the instruments at Thunderhook had limitations.
Viewing closely the surface of a tiny planet whirling at
frenzied speeds around a tiny sun buried somewhere within
the pulsing mass of the microcosm was a feat of photography
virtually beyond calculation. Shots of this section were few
and not too good. A few black dots across a landscape would
hint at the movement of a herd of animals.

"Plainly this form of photography, taken by telescope at high speed, just wasn't sufficient to show up any details," said Warren.

"That's understandable," said Marge. "It's a miracle they could get any scenes at all. But I don't understand how they can know so much now. How, for instance, can they get details today that will give them any discoveries of any inhabitants. . . ."

They thumbed through more photos. By the third year, the micro-universe was passing into a different phase of evolution—and moving relatively faster in that line even than our own universe. They saw that the spiral had assumed its present shape, and they saw from the notations, that the telephotography had concentrated conveniently on a few dozen stars and their systems in the outer edges of the spiral.

Stanhope came over and looked over their shoulders. "It's interesting, you know," he remarked, "that the worlds we studied mostly are in the same general locations as our own Earth and sun is in our galaxy, on the outer edges."

Warren came to the next picture and gasped. It showed a scene on a planet, where in surprising clarity a set of primitive huts could be seen and tiny humanoid figures standing about them. "What a change!" he exclaimed.

"Oh dear," said Stanhope. "Why that's entirely out of sequence!" He hastily fingered the balance of the file, then withdrew several and rearranged them. "Whoever has been in here must have been taking copies of some of these later ones."

"A spy," said Warren. "There's no doubt of it."

"Yes," said Marge, "but tell me how you get this detail and clarity all of a sudden."

"Oh, that was when we perfected the slow-down," said Stanhope. "We realized that we were going to miss a lot of important things if we couldn't pin down the events on the planetary surface. About then Marco worked out a method of increasing the magnetic grip on the microcosm. By running it counter to the thrust of the spiral galaxy, we found that by the constant application of great energy we could literally slow down the micro-universe. Everything moves slower—not to its own knowledge of course, but strictly in relation to ourselves.

"By this means we are able to slow down the breakneck pace of its internal evolution for hours when necessary—but only at limited intervals. In such periods we can actually take scenes at the surfaces of planets and examine the internal goings-on of the cosmic structures.

"So we are now able to follow the actual development of intelligent life on many of these worlds. We are on the verge of some important things. . . ."

The rearranged sequence now began to show these marvels. They saw dinosaurian beasts and early mammals. They saw the developing intelligences of various species, until on a number of worlds manlike beings had come into existence. Finally they saw these nomadic bands of club-wielding creatures settle in specific planetary areas, begin to build shelters and cultivate fields.

At the present time they realized that in the microcosm many of its worlds had reached a point closely similar to that of our Earth. They saw worlds whose civilizations were Roman in nature, others still in barbarian state. The inhabitants of the worlds varied in various details; none were exactly human in the Terrestrial sense, yet all were definitely humanoid enough to pass. Some were furry, some tailed, a few had oddments such as crests or stumpy horns, but basically all had the biped upright structure that seemed required of intelligent species.

They saw a number of photos that were ascribed to visions that appeared around Thunderhook. They saw that various things of a nature similar to other manifestations in Coningo

County were phased vibrations brought about by the growing similarities of these micro-worlds to the Earth itself.

Then they came upon sheafs of notes, sandwiched in between photos. Warren was about to pass over these sheafs for later until his eye was caught by lines in one. He saw place names and personal names and references to historical events and culture patterns on what seemed to be a micro-world. He showed these to Marge.

"This is strange. How could they possibly know what languages are spoken on one of these worlds, by what names their inhabitants call themselves, what the historical events are? No kind of photography could show this. No kind of machine could detect what goes on in their minds and what they record of themselves!"

He turned to Stanhope, but that man was back in his dark room and a warning red light indicated he was hard at work in his developing tanks.

He started to read an account of the machinations of some barbarian monarch of a world describing itself as Chundra but listed as Planet 4 of NWE 61. Marge looked at it. "Didn't make much sense to me, until I noticed it was something like an ancient history course I took in my senior year in high school. I hated the teacher; she flunked me."

At that moment, Stanhope's light blinked off, and the man himself came out, yawning. "Time for supper, I believe. I'm half-starved, and I hope you are too."

Marge and Warren got up, put the file back in its folder and into its proper drawer. "Better be sure you lock up tight this time."

Stanhope nodded. "I'm going to have to talk to Enderby about this. This is bad, very bad. Spies could destroy all we are doing here . . ."

They left together for the main lodge. Outside it was already dark and the stars of the greater universe were shining down. Warren felt odd as he walked with the others across the dark grass. For an instant he wondered whether other eyes were looking down on them, recording *their* doings. But then, he thought, we know our universe is infinite

Did the inhabitants of the microcosm know theirs was not?

CHAPTER SEVEN

DURING THE next few days Marge and Warren fit themselves into the life of Project Microcosm. Marge worked in the photography lab with Stanhope and sometimes in the main dome itself with whomever was at the observation post. She turned out to have a surprisingly good grasp of the photographic techniques—whoever had pulled strings to get her on *People* was not entirely without conscience. A number of improvements in the usage of these instruments were suggested by her and proved practical.

Warren found himself immersed in the huge mass of records, readings, and plates in the records hall. There was a great deal to be done; curiously enough, Thunderhook was actually understaffed for the work it had amassed and a good historian was indeed a welcome necessity.

He found himself drafting a general history of the project and at the same time a popular history of the microcosm itself. The simple set of plates which had been shown them by Stanhope was one but hastily put together and needed much improvement. After the first day on the job, Warren realized he had drawn himself a full-time chore, and a fascinating one.

Yet as he worked he wondered occasionally at the unexpected finding now and then of what appeared to be detailed accounts of minute fractions of history of one or another microcosmic world. Each time the thought came to him that he hadn't found out how this was known. Some material of detail had been gathered from the mirages—but nothing like that.

He knew that the mirages themselves were recent phenomena. The microcosm had only now begun to catch up in its own evolutionary age with the greater cosmos of our skies. Basically the work of the project was soon to pass from the study of the past to the study of the future. And this shift was taking place now, planet by planet, in the microcosm.

It would appear that most of the worlds were entering Roman or Grecian phases. Several were in their medieval era, and a handful passing though industrialization. Such a one was the world that had evoked the vision on the mountainside.

The work was not arduous. The scientists were all dedicated to their tasks, attending the pulsing microcosm like acolytes of a temple, as, in a sense, they were. Steiner and Marco alternated in charge of the tiny universe itself, with Weidekind and Rendell in assistance. What Carter Williams' work was, and that of the other member of the scientific staff, a man named Daniel Hyatt, was not yet clear to Warren. At no time were all present at meals, and he noticed that the men did not usually discuss their work then. The three guards were usually somewhere around.

Jack Quern and Mike Kenster seemed to be making eyes at Marge; it was evident that the girl had no objections at all to this interest. Either instinctively, or because she was quite accustomed to the attention of men, and was inclined to be flirtatious, she was clearly beginning to play one guard against the other. The members of the scientific staff watched

the play with amusement, but the girl seemed to have no
particular concern for them after working hours.

Warren smiled quietly when he saw Jack and Marge taking a stroll two evenings later. The girl plainly knew how to
handle men. As for Warren, he felt no particular interest in
her. True, he did feel that she was a sort of charge, having
come in with him on the same assignment, but he realized
that trying to maintain a paternal attitude toward the girl
—though in fact he was but slightly her senior—would get
him nowhere.

Enderby, as general manager, could usually be found a-
round the place, anywhere and everywhere. There were others
about—but they evidently had separate quarters and eating
arrangments—housekeeper, gardener; the men who attended
to the atomic pile; and others.

As for the spy problem, there was no further evidence of
this. Warren discussed this with Enderby, who had been in-
formed of the strange doings in the photo lab. Enderby was
disturbed, but pointed out that the spy was hardly likely to
sabotage an experiment whose successful working out was
necessary to his own operations. "I've notified the Foundation," said Enderby, "and they're going to see what they
can do about it."

After lunch on the third day, Warren and Marge started
off toward the records hall together. As they crossed the
grass, the girl turned and grasped his arm. "What's that
little dome against the side of the main one?" she asked
pointing.

Warren looked. Sure enough he noticed that there was a
sort of small bubble emerging from the side of the hemispherical building. He had seen it before, but simply never gave
it a thought. The bubble was built of the same cement but
seemed to have a newer look, as if it had been thrown up
and cut into the bigger structure as an afterthought. There
was a closed door leading into the small annex.

"Shall we take a look?" asked Warren and the two started towards it. When they reached it, Warren turned the handle of the door. It opened and they looked into a small round room.

They entered into darkness. At first they saw nothing—a heavy table near the door, a sheaf of writing paper on it, a metal ruler, a dozen sharpened pencils and a chair.

In the dark depths there was a faint light as if coming from a thick glassy aperture. They started over to it, and heard a groan.

"It's a man!" gasped Marge.

Lying on a wooden frame, just under the aperture against the far wall, a man seemed to be moving his head back and forth, muttering and groaning every now and then.

The two went over to him. "He's strapped down!" said Marge shocked. "And it's Carter Williams," added Warren.

"But what's the matter with him?" Marge whispered as the two leaned over. Carter was naked to the waist, and thick leather straps encircled his chest and strapped his arms and legs down to the frame of the hard flat bed. His eyes were closed but his lips were drawn up as if in agony and he was moving restlessly against the straps.

"He was all right at breakfast," said Warren softly. "I saw him at the table. He seemed in good health and in fine spirits."

"I know," murmured Marge breathlessly. "Jack told me that the spy would strike soon. I'll bet the spy caught Williams, knocked him out and tied him up here. We'd better release him quickly and get him some medical attention. Maybe he can tell us who did it to him!"

Warren whistled. "We'd better get him loose anyway—he looks as if he's in pain."

He bent over the moaning scientist and hastily unbuckled the straps.

Warren rubbed the thrashing man's forehead. "Williams!" he called. "Wake up! You're all right. Help's here!"

Williams's eyes opened. For an instant they stared at Warren, but as if without any recognition. Williams looked at him open-mouthed, then put out a hand, struggled to a sitting position.

Sitting up the young scientist rubbed his hand against his forehead, muttered something to himself. Again he looked around, as if seeing everything for the first time.

"Are you all right?" asked Warren. "Shall we get you medical attention?"

Williams's eyes widened, then he jumped up with unexpected force and grabbed Warren. The reporter fell back, almost losing his balance. Before he could recover himself, Williams's hands were on his throat, and the scientist was yelling furiously in some strange language.

Marge screamed. Williams turned quickly, glanced at the girl. Taking advantage of the distraction, Warren brought his fist up hard and buried it in Williams's mid-section. Again the scientist yelled, let go his grip on the reporter's throat.

Williams jumped back, yelled again in some outlandish gibberish, dashed around the room and grabbed the metal ruler from the desk. Brandishing this, he advanced, shouting unintelligibly.

The reporter dodged away from the swinging ruler. Marge, momentarily behind the crazed scientist, ran out the door and shouted for help.

It was probably but a minute more before help came, but to Warren, facing the madman, it seemed an hour. He managed just to keep out of Williams's reach; the metal ruler, wildly swinging and slashing through the air, missing him by fractions of an inch.

Then Kenster dashed in, this time a welcome sight, followed by Enderby.

The big guard grappled Williams from behind, wrapped

his arms around the scientist's until the man was helpless in the guard's grasp. Enderby circled around Williams until he faced him, then suddenly slapped him in the face and shouted his name.

The figure of the scientist seemed to sway, then became limp. His face cleared. The fury and stress that had stamped his features vanished. He closed his eyes a moment and opened them again. Now he recognized Enderby.

"Hello, Doc," said Williams in a quiet rational voice. "That was sudden. Who's holding me?"

At a nod from Enderby, Kenster let go his grip. Williams dropped his arms, smiling apologetically at Warren who was staring at him, puzzled. "Looks like I gave you a scare. But it wasn't I who was doing it. You should never have released those straps. Hyatt was to have called me in another half hour."

"But—but I don't understand," said Warren. "It seems to me that you were out of your mind."

"He certainly was," said Marge. "Completely batty, I'd say."

"No, no," smiled Williams. "You see, you weren't dealing with me. You were actually fighting with a captain of the Imperial Guard of Gwath-modr—an empire on Planet Two of NNW two sixty-five. I imagine he got quite a shock waking up here to find himself a prisoner of strange beings like us."

"Huh?" said Warren and Marge together.

Enderby laughed suddenly. "Of course! We must have forgotten to tell you about this. We'll have to explain. But Williams, you'd better get to writing up your memories before they fade."

The scientist nodded. "Yes. I've had a fascinating four months. Rugged, but colorful." He walked over to the deck, sat down, selected a pencil and began writing.

Enderby nodded towards the exit and they all trooped out without further talk. Kenster took his leave and went back.

Enderby, Warren and the girl stood just outside the little chamber.

"I don't follow," said Marge. "He said four months—but he was here at breakfast and at supper last night, too."

Enderby nodded. "Yes, he was at breakfast with us here, but between breakfast and now he has spent four months on a microcosmic planet. Actually it probably took longer than the last hour and a half."

"I thought nobody could actually penetrate the microcosm," said Warren, "yet now you say he has been there."

Enderby answered, "Both statements are correct. Nobody can penetrate the micro-universe physically, but it is possible to visit it *ex persona*. Come into the main dome and I'll explain."

He led the way to the hemisphere of the microcosm. Once there, standing before the everchanging marvel of the vast black, star-strewn global space, anything began to seem possible.

Enderby pointed to the various telescopes set up around the outer balcony. "It was an accident that led to our discovery of the means of transposing minds with inhabitants of the microcosm. One day, about two months ago, Rendell came on duty to find Weidekind slumped before a telescope, unconscious. When he did not respond at once to ministration, I was called. Between us we finally managed to bring Weidekind back to consciousness.

"He told us that he had been studying a particular planet on which we suspected intelligent life to have reached a fair state of advancement. He had slowed down the microcosm with the heaviest application of magnetic drag possible, in order to attempt to make some particularly detailed photographs on this particular planet which occupied an outer-fringe sun readily visible.

"He was focusing on this world very carefully, straining his mind to the task. Then he said he felt suddenly dizzy, felt himself more or less drawn, as in hypnotic trance, to the vision he was seeing. His instrument at that moment was focused on a mass of markings we believed to be a city on one of that world's continental land masses. He said he felt as if he could not take his eye away, as if he was being sucked into it.

"His thoughts became jumbled, and for an instant it was as if two minds were mingling in his own. Then there was a moment of complete blankness and when his eyes again came into focus, he found himself standing in the street of a completely alien city and under a completely strange sky.

"To make it short, he found himself suddenly occupying the body and mind of a manlike inhabitant of a city on that microcosmic world. He could understand all that he saw and heard because he was in full possession of that being's memory, language cells, and abilities. He knew his name, his position, his home, his duties, his life and memories. And to put it simply, for the next full year he lived that being's life!

"He was like a man who seizes control of another's car, only to find the road he must take permitting little if any deviation. He could observe, he could take some minor control, but it was as if most of his real self had been left behind.

"When we brought him back to consciousness, only a short time had passed, during which Weidekind's body was comatose. We know now that the mind of the alien being was occupying it, yet in this instance it was evidently unable to cope with or control Weidekind's human body. This happens occasionally in such transferals. Yet in this short interval, the planet had run through a full year of its development.

"Weidekind remembered most of his experience. He was able to write out the history of those twelve months of alien life; he was able to remember most of what he had known of the people he had visited, their history, legends, customs, hopes. As it happened they were in an interesting phase, one that corresponds to the very dawn of our recorded history, something like what it must have been at such places at Mohenjo-Daro and Akkad.

"We determined that what had happened was a phasing of sympathetic natural vibrations, along the same principle as the visions observed hereabouts. Only here, it was a deliberate phasing—two minds of rather similar outlook, of about equal intensity, simply phased each other."

Enderby stopped, looked into the microcosm. Warren and Marge had been listening intently. "And from that hypothesis you have worked out this system and use it regularly?" he asked though he knew the answer already.

Enderby nodded. "Yes, we worked it out to a practical system. It's quite strenuous to the mind—we find it dangerous to attempt more than once every other day. And sometimes the alien mind occupying the body of our transferee may be able to control it. He could do great damage in the hour or two he'd be at large, so we worked out the method of strapping a body down before the transfer was accomplished, and giving a sedative as well. The little chamber attached to this globe is our transferal room.

"Our explorer is attuned to the planet in question; he concentrates upon its surface Under hypnosis we increase his capacity and his drive to merge. If a mind exists that is capable of switching, the change occurs. Then when the reversal occurs, the experimenter immediately sits down and records all he can recall. We find that a delay in doing so causes a rapid fadeout of the knowledge—much like trying to remember a dream too long after awakening.

"We now have a regular pattern of transferals going on, mainly Williams and Hyatt, occasionally Weidekind and Rendell. The plain truth is that we can use more men in this work. There are so many worlds to visit and so many to check back on. These planets are passing through decades and centuries at vast rates. And these are the important years from the viewpoint of human parallels."

He looked at Warren with slightly arched eyebrows as he finished. The reporter stood silent, his thoughts in turmoil. It sounded intriguing, it sounded like the adventure of a lifetime, yet relatively harmless. Marge voiced the thought he was reluctant to express:

"What happens if the person on one of those worlds, whose mind you're occupying, dies or is killed? Who *really* dies?"

Enderby shrugged. "Frankly, we don't know. It hasn't yet happened, though there have been some narrow escapes. But still it's a chance that we'll have to take. It is right at this time that we may be able to start bringing back inventions not yet known to our own world; to make discoveries of undreamed-of practical value to human living."

The reporter smiled. "You know, Doc, visiting strange places is really my business. The other men here are not trained observers; I am. I'd like to be added to your list of regular transferees. So I'm volunteering here and now. When do I start?"

Enderby nodded. Marge looked from one to the other, gulped. "Golly . . . I think I'd like to take that cruise myself—just once, anyway; to see what it's like. I bet you could use a woman's point of view in your write-ups."

The old scientist glanced at her. "Quite possibly. I rather think you have a point there, Miss McElroy. Suppose you think it over. Anyhow, tomorrow, I'd like to give Alton a start at it." He glanced at his watch.

"Suppose you spend the rest of the afternoon going over the files on Planet Six of the SSW Twenty. I think we'd better look in on it without further delay. Tomorrow may be none too soon."

CHAPTER EIGHT

CARTER WILLIAMS and Enderby were waiting for Warren at the appointed time the next morning. He met them in the little chamber by the side of the main dome. He had studied the previous records of the planet he was going to visit, and was impressed by the spottiness of his knowledge.

There had been but two previous mental transfers there and the time lapse in microcosmic reckoning between each visit had been several hundred years. He knew that, judging by Terrestrial historical epochs, the inhabitants of that particular world should be somewhere in the same stage of existence as the Earth itself. That was, of course, providing that there had been no unusual setbacks, like geophysical disasters, or devastating post-medieval wars. He knew its earlier history in a general paleontological sense as well—in fact, he had seen photos of the very birth of the planet. In one sense he would come there as the most learned and knowing man on the planet; in a more immediate sense he would be among the most ignorant and least prepared.

It was to be an adventure the like of which—he realized —none had even dreamed. His whole career of a reporter in strange lands, of one who had taken notes amid the shots and flames of revolution, who had rushed into earthquake areas before the tremors had died, of reporting from up front in wars of distant lands—this career might, in a measure have prepared him. But also it might well be outdistanced within the next few minutes.

And yet of course he could be spending the next few microcosmic months—and months they'd be for him, even as a dream may seem to occupy days yet actually take but split seconds—merely in a dull and routine world, as a farmer plowing a field or a laborer in a mine. None knew what role he would find himslef occupying, or whose mind would come into tune with his.

Enderby injected into his arm a mild sedative which would rest his body while arousing his mental awareness. Warren lay down on the wooden bench and Williams strapped him down.

Now Enderby opened a little circular window on the wall over his head which gave into the dome within sight of the microcosm. An apparatus was wheeled over and fixed so that it caught a beam of light from the microcosm. Within the group of lenses the beam was clarified, enlarged and directed down into Warren's eyes. He looked into this apparatus and it was like looking into a telescope. He saw a star gleaming with several tiny dots of light attending it. This was the microcosmic sun whose designation was South South West sector 20. Now it enlarged rapidly and one of the attendant discs came more sharply into view—the sixth planet of that sun.

Warren watched the planet enlarge until it was a misty disc upon whose surface dark and light features could be seen—oceans and land masses. There was a crescent area of darkness where the day-night line showed. Warren saw that the planet had two moons, one large and brilliantly white, the other smaller and darker.

He felt drowsy and felt himself sinking into a foggy sort of awareness. The voice and sound of the two men standing near him faded and the apparatus itself faded away. Now only the planet hung in his view and he seemed to be hovering over it.

He became aware of a curious sensation as if somehow he were in two places at once—as if, impinging on his consciousness were other sounds, alien and unnatural. Suddenly there was a flash of pain, a sensation of unbearable pressure, a terrible roaring in his ears.

Everything went black.

Slowly he returned to consciousness. His hands and arms and legs began to feel sensation again, they were pressing still on the wooden frame of the bed and he felt the tight leather straps encircling his chest and legs. There was something binding his brow. He felt nauseous, and his ears were assailed by an odd pulsing humming.

Warren's first impulse was of disappointment. The transferal must have failed, for he could still feel the bench and the straps and could still hear the humming pulse of the microcosm. So, expecting to see Enderby hovering over him, he opened his eyes.

But there was no Enderby in sight. Instead he saw a brilliant glistening globe hanging before him in blackness. The larger satellite of Planet Six, he thought. The apparatus must still be focusing. He watched this moon for a while, wondering when the transferal was going to take place. But nothing seemed to happen.

Then it occurred to him that the vision of the moon was remarkably clear for a telescopic image refracted through several lenses from a moving microcosm. The satellite, in fact, was strikingly clear—he could see dark and lighter details against its glistening, brilliantly reflecting mass. It's a surface of ice, he thought, adding, of course it's the Ice Moon.

Aroused by sudden suspicion, he twisted his head, turned his vision, and gasped. He was not in the little room at all! He was somewhere else. But where?

There was no other person in sight. He was cooped up in a very tiny chamber, whose walls encircled him within a couple feet on every side. He moved his hands and found they were not strapped down. He raised his hands and felt the strap encircling his chest. He unbuckled it, unbuckled the brow strap that seemed holding his head back against the frame. He looked around.

He was half-reclining in a hard-framed seat, cushioned as if against shock. The pulsing humming sound was coming from below him. In the little chamber were tied-down boxes of equipment, a device for cooking food, a water purifier. He knew this without asking. In front of him was a board with strange controls beneath a wide window through which he was looking upon the Ice Moon.

For a moment he wondered how he seemed to know just where he was, and what he was doing. He knew that he was in the nose compartment of a nuclear-powered experimental rocket. He knew also that he was heading for the Ice Moon, with the object of making the first landing on it.

He knew . . . but there was a clicking on the board, and a voice spoke near him. "Are you there? Base calling Commander Wool-house in Kah-one. Please report."

Without thinking, he threw a switch on the board. "Wool-house reporting. All is well. Everything in running order."

"Congratulations, Dau! The Director of the Council sends his personal regards. We're all watching you and waiting for you! How are things up there?"

As Warren's voice began to reply, he sensed a part of his mind was sitting back astounded. The transferal had been a success. The mind of Warren Alton was now that of some being calling himself Dau Wool-house—this last name was in the native language, of course, but this language was entirely familiar to the brain Warren occupied. This Commander was a rocket pilot—was, in fact, the man selected by the military forces of his country, the Counciliary Democracy of Souva on the planet Komar, to be the Columbus of Space for that world.

This rocket trip to the Ice Moon of that planet was the result of dozens of years of rocket research, of design and trial, of stratosphere shots, of sub-satellites, and manned rocket planes, and of unmanned robot rockets to the Ice Moon and the Stone Moon as well.

Now Warren/Dau recalled the months of arduous training he had undergone. He recalled his selection from the many qualified volunteers, and how proud he'd been of his selection. It seemed to him that he was a curious mixture. The brain of the Komarian could and did respond naturally and easily to what was expected of him. But Warren's own mind seemed to be both part of and separate from that brain. He could direct it if he wanted, or he could let it guide him by its acquired memories and knowledge. It was roughly as if, dreaming in a deep sleep, he was aware, without waking, that he was dreaming.

At a request from the base, he began to read off the dials on his board, reporting back. He replied to messages with ease and confidence, recalling each person as they spoke to him.

But, Warren asked himself, why this particular man? Then he realized that the answer to that lay in his own nature. On Earth, Warren Alton was an adventurer, a seeker of strange places; on Komar, Dau Wool-house was of a similar inclination. Both men had been strapped to frames at the same split-instant, both had been subjected to strange tensions.

What more natural then that their two minds had phased in chemical sympathy?

At a thought, Warren looked down at himself. What sort of being was he? He knew something of the Komarians, but searching his new brain and glancing at his body, he brought back to mind the nature of the Komarians. They were human, yes. He was, he judged by memory, the equivalent of six feet tall. He was bald, as were all Komarians, and had but four fingers to each hand. His eyes were slanted and blue, his ears round and flat. He was wearing a one-piece flying suit, pressurized against space. But he was otherwise quite distinctly of the human family as those on Earth knew them.

He remembered his parents, he knew his family; he recalled his girl friend, lovely by Komarian standards—she had a particularly attractive mane of hair running from the back of her neck to the base of her spine—a female attribute of special beauty. . . .

The voice on the radio beam spoke again. It was inquiring after him personally; did he feel well? Was he dizzy, and so forth. Warren reassured his listener on these subjects, and quietly began to describe the Ice Moon as seen from his position.

He was coming in on this satellite for a landing, the first such landing ever to be made. The satellite was the largest of those of Komar. That planet was a world of Earthly size, judging strictly by local analogies. There were giant gaseous planets in the system of the same type as Jupiter and Saturn. By comparison with these, Komar was a solid world, smaller and warmer—an Earth-type "inner" planet. It had two moons; one stony and fairly small and distant; the other larger—a thousand miles in diameter if you considered Komar as seven thousand—and apparently a huge mass of ice, a ball of frozen water which possibly might have a rocky core.

Landing on it was important. Whatever nation could establish control of it might well prove the victor of the planet Komar. Warren searched Dau's brain and he was able to add to the missing centuries in Komarian history as known on Thunderhook. There had indeed been an industrial revolution as scheduled, and that world now found itself with two leading nations, both with rudimentary atomic power. One was a democracy, the other an oligarchy. Each distrusted the other, each feared war, but found peace untenable. And each thought that possession of the Ice Moon meant an end to the threat of conflict.

Warren rode the rocket for two days. During this time he

began to live the role of Dau so well that for periods he virtually forgot who he had been. Yet, searching space outside the rocket, he was impressed again with the reality of this other universe, as compared with that in which Earth existed. He saw on all sides a depth of black space sprinkled with stars. He saw that the stars were thick and heavy near the center of the galaxy, and that they thinned out on the opposite side. He saw the several planets of Sun 20 glowing in their orbits, he saw a comet, and his instruments recorded meteors—the last remnants of the cosmic dust of creation. He saw Komar shining warm and homelike across a wide field on one segment.

With his knowledge of the universe of Earth and Sol, Warren strained his eyes to the darkest section of the space around him, but no evidence was there of this other universe surrounding. And he began to wonder just what was the true relationship between the two universes.

Steiner had insisted that the microcosm was truly as large as the entire Milky Way galaxy, that its enclosure within the space of the dome on Thunderhook was only relative—that it was a sort of illusion or optical concentration on a small break in space-time. Steiner had argued that a mile inside the microcosm was fully the equal of a mile outside it . . . and this never had made sense.

But how could Warren doubt it now? Concentrate as he would, he could not dispute that his present body, the rocket he rode, the planet he'd left and the satellite for which he headed, were—so far as he could tell—made of molecules and atoms of exactly the same chemical and electronic values of those of the universe he had left. Science said that a molecule of carbon is a molecule of carbon, regardless of where and when. The carbon molecules of the microcosm had to be exactly the same size and quality and have the same properties as those of the outer universe. If that didn't make sense, it was merely due to the limitations of the human mind.

As he lived and breathed the life of Dau Wool-house, Warren Alton was forced to acknowledge that indeed this man was every bit as alive and normal and valid as the reporter for *People*. What, then, *was* reality?

Reality, Warren considered, lies in the sizes of these universes. Ours is infinite, this is finite. We have thousands of mighty galaxies; this, but one.

On this thought he searched the outer skies through the rocket's telescope for those glimmering spirals of light that marked such galaxies as those of Andromeda—but he found none. Searching Dau's memory of school, he recalled the philosophical arguments that waxed hot in the colleges of Komar: Was the universe infinite and endless, or was it finite and curved on itself in space?

The rocket was swinging around the Ice Moon now, braking itself by assuming an orbit, gradually narrowing the distance to the glistening surface of ice. Looming high were great mountains, upthrust peaks of ice reaching thousands of feet into the satellite's airless sky. There were huge crevasses and chasms, where the ice shield that had coated the moon in some distant past had buckled and split. There were starspray cracks where meteors had smashed into the ice surface.

The closer one came the more striking the view; it was a landscape of desolation and wonder, the rays of the sun constantly breaking into rainbow auras that mingled in a hundred different spectra as the light struck the crags and tossed surfaces of the moon.

As he closed in for the final landing, Warren saw something else in the field. There was a glimpse of light and a flash of fire far off in the view, and he strained his eyes against the glow of the ice world. There was another rocket coming in for a landing—another rocket where there could not be one!

He called back to Komar for instructions, but he was so close to the Ice Moon that he could not hear the answer. He decided to ignore that other rocket until he made his landing.

His rocket closed in, swooped lower and lower, and now slid just over the peaks of a viciously sharp upthrust of mountainous ice and down onto a wide hundred-mile field of shining ice. Down lower and lower he arced and knew as he did so that his rocket was intended to land that way—not tail-down, as Earth rockets were supposed to land on Luna. No, for this moon, the giant runners that ran about the body of his rocket would do the trick.

Now the rocket slid gently down on the ice, its runners touched, bounced, touched again, and then the rocket was whizzing across the ice like a bullet. Desperately Warren held the controls, riding the tobogganing spacecraft across the endless horizon of white glassy ice. He saw a crevice appear before him, a spurt of the rocket power lifted the craft over it and set it down again. He twisted the controls, spun the rocket around until he was facing the rear and the rocket racing backwards, and now he fired his rockets in quick short spurts. The sliding craft began to brake rapidly, was brought to a proper halt, and Warren was congratulating himself on a good landing when suddenly there was a jarring crash. Warren was thrown from his seat, as the bulkhead behind him seemed to cave in on him. He heard a grinding noise, a tearing of metal, and he hit the front windshield with a bang.

He picked himself up dizzily in a moment. Plainly he must have struck against something unforeseen, some upthrust in the ice, an invisible obstacle in this supposedly flat ice field. Quickly he looked himself over; he was all right, save for a bruise on his forehead, and a skinned hand. He sniffed, but the little cabin was still airtight. There was no telltale hiss of air escaping. He glanced at the board but it had stopped functioning as far as the engines were concerned. He depressed switches but could get no reaction.

He opened the little cabinet and took out his pressure suit. Rapidly he dressed himself in it, in the tight compression of the bands and the form-fitting suit which would keep him warm and keep his body under normal pressure. The helmet went on tightly, the airtank fit. All set, he pushed open the door that led into the middle section, where a now-empty fuel tank would become his airlock section. As he pushed the door open, there was a whoosh of air. The rest of his ship was no longer airtight, that was clear. He saw that the outer metal skin of the middle compartment had buckled. Through it he could see twisted tubes and great splinters of jagged ice thrust inside.

The lock door was bent in the middle but he forced it open and stepped out on the surface of the Ice Moon. He was the first man to set foot on another world—but likely it would be some other that would bear the honor, for honors do not go to those who do not return.

Around him the sky was still obscured by the cloud of ice dust that had been sprayed by the collision. It was hanging in the airless space, slowly drifting to the ground in the light gravity of the small world.

He felt giddy himself, realized his weight was slight. He turned around and surveyed the rocket.

The entire rear, the engines and tubes were smashed like an eggshell. The tobogganing rocket had slid into a mass of broken ice directly in its path. It had crumpled. There could be no repairing its engines.

Warren tramped around the rocket examining it, confirming the damage. He saw that there was a chance he might be able to hitch up one or two of the dislodged batteries and get his cabin elements functioning—maybe even get off a communication to Souva.

Food he had—the collision might break it up, but that wouldn't render it inedible—if he could manage to defrost it.

Warren stood and looked up at Komar and his Dau memories were shocked and sad. To have made it, yet to have lost at the same time. But—he smiled—in any case, Souva would get the honor of claiming the Ice Moon. He searched inside the wrecked stores of the rocket and found what he was seeking: a light titanium pole bearing at its top the standard of Souva. He dragged this out, bent it straight where it had been twisted in the crash, and, walking out a little way from the rocket, stood it up and forced it into the ice.

He stood back and saluted. The standard of the nation of Souva stood there proudly, the five-rayed sun of gold with the clasped hands of blue and orange superimposed.

He went back to the rocket and looked again. And this time, somehow, the standard looked lost and small against the black sky and the cold hard brilliance of the icy landscape. The stars shone down in burning splendor and the world of Komar appeared soft and glowingly warm. Against these the standard now suddenly seemed only a childish toy.

As Warren stood there in the cracked door of his rocket, before beginning the task of trying to rig up his electric system, the other rocket came into view. He saw the yellow flame of its exhaust just over the edge of the mountain top; he saw it flaring down for a sliding landing on the same field of flat ice that had deceived Warren.

He stood and gaped in astonishment. He could not take his eyes off the other rocket. It came on down, angled towards the ice, hit in a nice sliding run, skated on long runners across the ice leaving a cloud of ice particles like a trailer behind it.

He saw the rocket begin to swing about, to reverse itself on its runners, just as Warren had done, and suddenly Warren himself could not suppress a cry, "Look out!"

But the driver of the other rocket could not hear him. For at the instant of the shout, the nose of the other rocket brushed against the ice, the rocket dipped sharply and skidded along on its nose for another thousand feet before spinning to a stop.

Warren began to run across the ice in great bounds, aided by the light gravity, toward the other rocket, possibly two miles away.

He ran on, leaping small cracks, sliding madly on the icy surface, and as he ran he strained his eyes. Now a figure climbed from the bent and broken nose of the other rocket; he saw a bulkily space-suited figure stumble as if in pain across the ice. The figure was carrying something.

Warren skidded to a halt, perplexed. Was this rocketeer carrying a weapon? He realized that of course he was being foolish running to the aid of an enemy. This man must be from Tannok, from the odious oligarchy. Perhaps he would be fired on.

The other figure stumbled to a halt, swung the object he was carrying and stuck it upright in the ice. Warren gasped. It was the Tannok standard, of course. He should have realized: the infamous Duk-Duk bird with its talons grasping a three-pronged star!

Suddenly the whole thing struck Warren as unbearably funny. Two hopelessly wrecked rocket pilots, without a chance of returning to Komar, planting their silly symbols on a frozen world that had no use for either of them. Two emblems of the quarrels of planet-bound worms, trying to pretend that their petty differences mattered here.

He burst out in uncontrollable laughter and staggered forward. And finally the other figure came to him, and when

they met, Warren saw that the stranger was equally hyster-
ical. They fell into each others' arms, roaring with laughter
and crying at the same time.

CHAPTER NINE

"We were on the Ice Moon for three full months before we
finally managed to get back. The engines and tanks of the
Tannok ship were in good condition, the nose and living
quarters of mine were likewise. We moved the broken nose
of his and welded on the front of mine. It took three months
to complete the job"

Warren's voice, relating his experiences, was holding
everyone spellbound. It was late in the evening, supper had
been finished and the great living room in the lodge was
mainly dark, save for the flickering of logs in the old fireplace.
Around the big table were most of the staff of Thunderhook,
all fascinated

These were men who had heard many stories of strange
worlds, but this time they knew they had passed over a line
into something different. Warren's adventure was the first to
go into a scientific achievement beyond those of Earth itself.
He was the first human who had experienced—even though,
in a sense, at second-hand—actual space flight and actual
conditions on uninhabitable worlds.

Marge was there in the big room, but she had taken herself over to a corner by the fireplace and was exchanging
whispers with the off-duty guard, Jack. Steiner and Hyatt

were on duty. But the others had spent the hour after the table had been cleared listening to Warren.

"Why the laughter? Why the amity between the two antagonists?" asked Weidekind. "I don't understand what you two had in common. Didn't you both owe everything to your own nations?"

Alton pursed his lips. "It's hard for me to explain it now," he said, "but at the time it was quite clear. Somehow being so far away from the home world made its politics petty. It was the outer view. It wasn't a loss of patriotism or anything like that—rather, it was a new and greater sort of pride, a sort of planetary pride. We were both proud simply of being men and being from Komar. We had, you see, so much more in common with each other than with any conceivable thing or object on the Ice Moon where we had landed.

"Our act of planting our standards was sort of a conditioned reflex, you see. It was an act we had each thought of before ever starting our trip; but when we actually did it, it seemed so silly! You see, there was our home world right up there in plain sight in the sky, so much more awesome, so much *vaster* somehow than our silly little standards, representative of conflicting superstitions and the fossilized angers of long-dead ancients. On top of that, it was so obvious to us both that we were as good as dead. We had both cracked up, neither of us could return. Why fight?

"It wasn't until afterwards that we thought we could make the return trip up by patching one good ship out of two wrecks. If the gravity hadn't been so light there, we probably couldn't have achieved it. But we had nothing else to do and only a few months' limited supply of air and food—so we tried, and succeeded.

"By the time we returned to Komar in our hybrid rocket the whole planet had had plenty of time to follow our adventures. Our names were on everyone's mind and mouth.

We outshone all the petty political troubles, all the border disputes, all the selfish mutual distrusts of our nations.

"And we ourselves saw what a chance had been given us. When we returned, we landed in a neutral nation, famous on Komar for its skill in effecting international arbitration and peace. We asked the leaders of our own countries to come to us—and they did. They had to, public pressure was so strong on them to do so after our return. Then we gave them our new philosophy. Out in space, Komar was our world and against the other regions of space, we were and could only be Komarian—not Souvans or Tannoki.

"I don't know what will come of it in the history of Komar, because I blanked out in the middle of a triumphal tour the next month. That's when I came to here—after just about seventy of our minutes had passed since the transferal started."

There was quiet at the table. Then several started discussing it at the same time. Some seemed to understand the viewpoint, others insisted that it must have been an idiosyncracy of the Komarian mind. Enderby finally rapped on the table. "Time to retire, men; we still have work ahead of us."

As the staff began to leave, Enderby turned to Warren. "Did you finish writing up the details of your experience? Have you gotten the data on that rocket ship down—its engine, its fuel and mechanism? This is actually the very first new invention to come out of our microcosm. It's extremely important!"

Warren nodded. "I have most of it down on paper, Chief. I'll complete it in my room before I go to sleep. I don't want any of the details to fade from my memory."

Enderby nodded agreement. They began to drift out to their separate quarters. Warren went up to his bedroom on the second floor of the lodge, sat at his writing desk there and worked for another three hours on his manuscript, detailing exactly what he could remember. He was able to describe the rocket ship minutely—having had three months of actual work in taking one apart and putting another together. He was able to sketch out the wiring, the fitting and sizes of the rockets and their chambers, the fuel consumption and the nature of the fuel itself. As he worked, he was aware that some of the details would prove eye-openers to modern Terrestrial engineers. There were clever short cuts, there were hookups that would solve some difficult problems of rocketry; and the fuel itself was revolutionary.

By midnight he was through. He could expand on the notes next day, but now it was basically all there. He yawned, undressed, and putting out the light went to bed.

Sometime later he opened his eyes. The room was dark, it was still deep night. Something had disturbed him. He lay silent and then heard a faint squeaking, a tension of changing floor boards. He strained his ears and fancied he could hear breathing, then the squeak came again as if someone were stealthily trying to cross his floor on bare feet.

He sat up, started to get out of bed. There was a very faint light from the stars coming through his open window that showed a dark shadow bulking near the door; something that had no place there.

"Who's there?" he called. And instantly the shadow darted forward. Warren sprang out of bed, rushed to meet it.

A fist crashed a glancing blow against his head. Warren swung, felt his hand brush someone's shoulder. He grabbed for the stranger, but another fist struck him in the chest and then the stranger hurled him away with force and turned.

Warren lunged after him, but his hand on the stranger's back slipped and in another moment the unknown was out of the door and gone. Warren leaped to the door, which had been left open, and looked down the hall. He could see no one. Somewhere a door snapped shut and the building was silent.

Warren closed the door of his room and snapped the light

on. On his desk his pile of papers, the manuscript of his experiences, had been brushed to the floor, as if the intruder had picked it up, but dropped it when Warren had interrupted him.

The reporter picked up the manuscript, leafed through the pages putting them in order. None was missing. He sat down in thought. Enderby was right in assuming they were important, and Stanhope's evidence of a spy was now corroborated in full. Someone at Thunderhook was keeping a private record of the project's discoveries—obviously for transmission somewhere else.

There was no doubt that in this rocket material there were military advantages to be gained. From this point on, discoveries would come from the microcosm which would be of immense beneficial signficance for mankind—but which might disclose to an unscrupulous possessor technological secrets that would give such a party—or such a nation—world mastery.

He made sure his door was locked and the manuscript tucked under his mattress before he went to sleep again that night. In the morning he sought out Enderby and taking him aside told him what had happened.

The old scientist was greatly disturbed. He agreed that precautions had not been adequately taken to safeguard the data of the project.

Later that day, during the lunch break, Enderby announced a new set of regulations. From now on all data relating to new discoveries was to be deposited with him to be placed in the safe. A guard would be on hand at all times to cover this. New locks would be placed on the records-hall doors and windows, and every man was warned to take careful precautions with anything that might be of value.

This announcement set forth further discussions on the nature of the work ahead. There was a meeting of the leaders, Enderby, Steiner, Marco and the others. One of the results of this was the decision to allot specific planets to specific men. As Warren had been involved so well with Komar, he would henceforth transfer to that planet regularly, rather than drift around the microcosm. In this way, a certain specialization could be achieved. Weidekind, for instance, would have another world—the one where the battle of tanks had miraged on the mountainside. Williams was assigned to the world that had once harbored the empire of Gwath-modr. Hyatt, a world near the center of the micro-galaxy whose inhabitants were also pushing close to space flight. And Rendell, still another.

Further, they would try to keep contact with these respective worlds at least two or three times a week—and so try to keep the histories from having too great lapses. Twice a week might well mean a thousand years between eras, or even more, depending on whether the microcosm was being magnetically braked or not.

It was further agreed that every two days a conference would be held of all transferees to co-ordinate their knowledge and to build up the history of the microcosm. Up to now they had been dealing with isolated worlds emerging from the original magma and passing through the same stages of evolution known to Earth. Now they were passing into stages that lay in Earth's future and so the discoveries and histories would be of immense value in charting the probable future course of human life on Earth and in our own infinite universe.

On the next day, Warren was ready to revisit Komar. He had expected to wait a third day but it was the opinion of the staff that results of the opening of the space age be charted at not too great a gap.

Warren again was strapped to the frame, again injected, again found the focusing device bringing before him the telescopic presentation of Komar and its neighboring planets.

There was a moment of dizziness, a period of blackout, of sharp vertigo.

Then he heard a voice speaking in rolling sonorous tones. He recognized standard phrases of glittering generalities, references to "our glorious traditions," and other over-familiar terms. In his mind he knew these statements should be thrilling, for they were obviously appeals to pride and glory. Yet he found himself indifferent. They were clichés, dull, tarnished word combinations that had all but lost meaning.

His eyes were closed, so he opened them. He was sitting in a room, and the voice was speaking from somewhere within it. He turned his head and saw in full color the face and shoulders of a man on a screen. A television set, before which were sitting in rapt interest a woman and two young boys. The woman, he knew, was his wife, the boys his children. They were listening because they were proud of their father and the event that was about to transpire.

Warren's Komarian mind knew what was coming, supplied the answers. But Warren himself, occupying that brain, was excited. His excitement took hold of the host's brain and the man moved his chair around and watched the speaker.

The speaker was Fod Stone-gorge, the present Chairman of United Komar. The occasion was very special for two reasons. First, it celebrated the Five Hundredth Anniversary of the opening of the Space Age, and the same occasion was the announcement of the imminent launching of the first expedition into stellar space.

The whole of Komar was excited, and he remembered that before the Chairman had come on, delegates had spoken briefly from each of the six planetary colonies of Komar. These colonies—two of which were now fairly populous on worlds with large arable land masses, and the other four of which were domed-in mining centers on inhospitable and airless satellites—were the pride of Komarian civilization, which was now on a world basis.

Now Fod Stone-gorge paused dramatically, his plump cheeks quivering, the perspiration on his bald head gleaming. He waved a finger at the audience, comprising the entire population of the planet, and made the announcement.

The starship was ready. It would take off for the nearest star in three days. Its crew had been selected with care. They would sail it out beyond the farthest planet, under the newly developed cosmic ion drive. Approaching the speed of light, they would hurl the ship through the six light-years to the nearest star, make their landing, survey it, and return. The crew would be placed in suspended animation during that time so that the trip would be tolerable to them. They could be expected back in about forty years' time.

All this Lo Brake-hold knew perfectly well. His family knew it, too, for they had had months to reconcile themselves to his loss. Lo was the man in whose body Warren's ego had been transferred, and Lo was one of the twelve crew members of the starship.

To Lo the speech was only another dread milestone before the day of departure. He was willing; he had been selected by test—a spaceman of great experience. His family had acquiesced. As a matter of fact, Lo's wife would go into special suspended animation at a local hospital and be kept under until his return. He would not lose his mate. As for his sons, they would go on, they would be fully matured men by his return.

The next three days passed in feverish activity After the announcement to the world, there were public exhibits of the starship; there were last minute preparations. Came the day, and Lo bade farewell to his wife, and went with the other eleven men to the spacefield.

Fod Stone-gorge was there himself. He was a typical pol-

itician, full of bombast and loud, meaningless words, thought
Lo Brake-hold—with Warren in agreement.

The starship, appropriately named the *Dau Wool-house*,
was strange. Warren now consciously exerted himself, began
to probe the Komarian mind for details of the ship. It was
a beauty. He saw now what the next five hundred years of
space flight would bring, saw the infinite developments and
ramifications of the rocket drive, the full application of nuclear power to the space-ship, the evolution of a synthetic
gravity within the ships. But this starship was still further advanced. Its drive was a new development, based on the
currents of cosmic rays between the worlds, and it would
not achieve its full speed until well beyond the outermost
planet. Then it would spread out something like sub-magnetic
sails—great invisible force nets for miles on every side. Thus,
catching cosmic particles, it would be drawn along in their
streams and rush like a leaf on them through the cosmos.

After the leave-taking and the speeches, came the take-
off. After the take-off, they were rocketing past the orbits of
the planets. After the last planet, a stony-cold, barren rock a
billion miles from the parent sun on which one lonely en-
closed observatory had been built as Komar's then-farthest
outpost, signaled its final good luck message.

Then the cosmic sails were unfurled. The charts within
the great ship showed the lines of force, and there was a
period of tension as the members of the crew wondered
whether they would find the streams of cosmic ions. Then
a twitch, then a rush, then they were off, moving faster and
faster across the black depths of empty space, heading on
toward the tiny sharp point of light, which was a sun six
light-years away. Their destination.

Lo Brake-hold saw all this from his post. And Warren's
mind wondered if Steiner had charted that distant star. If he
could go back now, for a moment, to Thunderhook, he might

anticipate what would be coming. Now the signal came for the crew to withdraw to quarters.

Lo lay down in the cocoon-like net that was waiting. It closed over him like a pod, it sealed him down. He felt a moment of panic, of suffocation. . . .

Warren opened his eyes suddenly and looked up. He was back in the little chamber next to the Dome. Above him the focusing apparatus was being wheeled away by Hyatt. Warren turned his head, said, "Wait."

Hyatt was startled. He gave him a look. "Why, a moment ago you were under. What's happened? I'd swear it took!"

Warren's eyes fell on the clock by the desk. It was exactly one minute since he had gazed originally into the telescopic image of Komar. One minute—and it was already fifteen days since he had arrived on that microcosmic world!

"Hyatt, hold it. In about an hour I want you to put me under again. Meanwhile get me unbuckled. I'll try to jot down the details of some marvelous space-flight inventions before they get blocked out."

Hyatt unbuckled him and he set to work, sitting at the desk and scribbling out the key secrets of the advanced rockets, of the nuclear drive, jotting down notes on the other technological items in the mind of Lo Brake-hold, star-explorer.

His immediate task finished, Warren resumed his position on the frame, and Hyatt adjusted the vision. It took but a glimpse of the star system itself, of the region of SSW 20 and vicinity, before Warren blanked out. He had but one momentary thought; he had, in his haste to put down what he knew, simply forgotten to ask Steiner for a briefing on star SSW 19—the place to be visited.

The blankness seemed to linger for a while. It was as if he were in deep sleep. Then gradually the sleep dissipated and became replaced by a feeling of great ennui, of pain in his joints and of fever. He opened his eyes and saw that the sleeping pod was open. He roused his Komarian body, and as Lo Brake-hold he stepped down.

It was painful waking up after eight years, and the rest of the crew felt much the same. It was perhaps a week before any of them felt fit. Vitamins, high-concentration diets, and special exercising machines brought them back to good shape after their long sleep.

The star was close. They saw its shining light large against the sky and they saw that it had three planets—two giant gaseous ammonia worlds, and one small hard-surfaced planet.

The small world was slightly less in diameter than Komar. It had a bearable atmosphere; its heat extremes were within Komarian toleration. After circling it for two days, the *Dau Wool-house* settled for a landing on a green and pleasant continent.

The crew looked out on meadows not too different from those of their home world. They saw no sign of large life, but they did see some insect forms.

A group went out, came back safely. Then Lo Brake-hold and five others went out, and trekked through the plain to the distant hills.

They toiled up the hills and came to caves. They looked into the caves, and saw things that appeared bright and shining. The things bright and shining also saw them—and came out to greet them. They were the bright and shining eyes of a band of creatures straight out of a Komarian nightmare.

They were beings twelve feet high, possessed of six multi-jointed legs, possessed of great beaked heads that snapped and probed for the strangers.

Two men were killed in the first attack then Lo and his companions destroyed the monsters with their hand atomic sprayers.

The four Komarians turned and trekked back to the ship,

but before they got there a band of manlike beings emerged from trap doors in the meadow. The trap doors were the surface entrances of the subterranean villages of the thinking beings of Planet 1 of SSW 19.

The four Komarians tried to parley with these manlike primitives, and for their efforts two more were killed. The atom sprayers cleared the meadow and the trap doors snapped shut in a flurry of terror by the primitives.

Lo and one other were almost back to the starship when a being flashed out of the sky like a hawk upon a helpless chick. This strange creature was something like a giant wasp and something like a huge dragonfly and a lot like a pterodactyl. It struck the only two beings on the whole planet foolish enough to walk in plain sight under the sunlight.

As Lo's life flickered out in the second of impact, he had just for a split second seen the defensive fire flicker from the guns of the *Dau Wool-house,* first starship of Komar. . . .

As Warren Alton sat up on the framework bed in the room next to the microcosm dome, he knew what would happen if he was within the mind of a man experiencing death. He'd awaken on Thunderhook Mountain with a splitting headache.

But headache or not, he wrote the story down, and told it that night to a spellbound audience in the main hall of Project Microcosm. The technical details of the star drive had, however, been locked safely away.

CHAPTER TEN

"So NOW WE KNOW what happens in the event of a death during transferals," said Steiner, clasping his hands together on the table as he leaned over the report of Warren

Alton's experience. "Our man simply returns to consciousness here."

They were seated around the main table in the afternoon next day, conferring on events in the microcosm. At this session they passed around each transferee's reports for the reading of every member of the team. The details of the various future inventions were separately recorded, but the general account of the development was set forth.

Marco disagreed with Steiner. "I am not sure that it is always necessary that it be that way. It seems to me entirely possible that under some circumstances the ego of the microcosm man temporarily phased into our Earth brain might simply remain—permanently overprinted due to shock and to the original power of the mind. We have been fortunate not to have a death occur during one of these visits, but we must not be surprised at anything. Remember, this transferal is mutual—and the universe of our making is on a full basis of equality with our particular section of this universe in which we live."

Enderby nodded. "Well, this all remains to be seen. An interesting speculation, but so far just that and nothing more. I see a more interesting development here." He stacked together the eight reports that had been turned in since their previous session, ruffled through them.

"Have you noticed how much these accounts have in common? Here we have visits to eight widely separated planets in this microcosm, eight out of a hundred thousand possibles, and yet of these eight inhabited worlds, seven have now worked out some form of space flight. Two have found techniques of star travel, and the rest are progressing along the same line.

"It seems to me that we have here a clear indication of the course of human society. We know that in the past these worlds passed through much the same sort of periods as our own Earth did—savagery, nomadic society, agricultural communities, slave-keeping societies, medievalism, the rise of industry, electric and atomic energy, the rise of a world viewpoint in place of varied national viewpoints, and now space travel.

"I think it obvious that all this points to a natural sequence in the movement of planetary intelligences. But I wonder what comes next? So far none of the inhabitants of these planets has yet met another. Star flight will undoubtedly bring that about in short order."

Warren chuckled. "My first experience was hardly conducive to star colonization. I wonder if anybody on that expedition ever got back?"

Williams laughed. "You'll find out, I think, soon enough. But the first star expedition from Diol—my world—was a success. I wasn't on it, though. Didn't have your luck, Warren. Read all about it on the news tapes while working behind a counter in a synthetic farming center."

Enderby smiled. "I have a feeling that events will move mighty fast. They've been jumping rather quickly each trip now. The long periods are over, when all we found were just savage tribes. Over for good."

Warren nodded. "We can't dare let any of these worlds go too long. Can't we put more men on?"

Enderby shook his head. "I really don't dare. Steiner and Marco must keep on with their astrophysical observations. They are also of value. Bear in mind that most of this transferal work is actually a side line, a by-product of the original purpose of this project."

"How about taking up Marge on her offer to transfer?" asked Warren. "She's interested. And she's not dumb by any means."

"But perhaps not too observant," said Enderby.

Warren waved a hand. "With all the planets that should be covered, what can we lose? Besides it might be valuable to get a female transferal, at least once. She did master photography, you know—she might prove quite apt along certain lines of that sort—perhaps a powerful visual memory."

Enderby glanced around. There were smiles on the other men's faces. Steiner nodded, Marco grinned; Weidekind, Williams, Rendell, Hyatt, all approved.

"That settles it," said Enderby. "Call in the girl and we'll get her started."

The meeting broke up. Warren went with Williams over to the records hall. Marge was at the developing tanks with Stanhope hovering nearby. She looked surprised when Warren told her.

"Golly!" she said. "That's wonderful! I didn't really think he'd ever give me a break. You fellows had all the fun. I'm starting now?"

At Warren's nod, she started out. "Oh, Lordy. I've got to fix myself up. My hair's a mess, and—"

"Hey," said Warren, "you're not really going anywhere. They'll never see you—not the *real* you. In fact the whole thing will be over in an hour or so."

"Maybe they'll never see the real me, but I'll think about it, just the same," the girl retorted. "After all, if you think I'm going to lie there unconscious, looking like something out of a circus side show, you'd better think again. After all, how do I know who's coming into this place while I'm a-sleep? Mr. Carlyle might even pop up for a visit!"

She took herself forthwith to her room, and came down fifteen minutes later, hair redone, lipstick renewed, a fresh dress on.

Once in the transferal chamber, she planked herself down, took the injection without even wincing. "Where to?" she asked.

"We're shooting blind," said Williams. "We've never had adequate photos or coverage of the packed center of the microcosmic galaxy. The stars are too densely packed there for good results from telephotography. So we're just going to aim your mind telescopically at the mass of central hub stars and let it rove until something phases. You're going to get a brand-new world all for yourself."

"Hey," she said, "you've got me a little uneasy now. I just wanted a nice comfortable, familiar world."

Warren shook his head, and resting a hand on her shoulder pushed her into a reclined position while Williams adjusted the viewer. In another moment she was raptly staring into the microcosm, into the great blazing mass of shining stars at its center. In another minute she had drifted off, as she lay recumbent and unconscious on the frame.

Warren and Williams sat in the little chamber, chatting while Marge remained quiet for the better part of an hour. Once or twice she mumbled something in an odd language. The rest of the time, she was still, her face pale and tense.

Once Jack Quern looked in, saw the girl and scowled. "Watcha using her for?" he asked. "She's a nice kid, but not for that kind of stuff. Taking advantage of her, that's what!"

"Okay," said Warren. "We aren't hurting her. She'll probably talk your ear off when she wakes up."

Jack nodded. "We got a date to go walking in the woods tonight after supper. There's a full moon."

Williams smiled when Jack left. "Romantic cuss, isn't he? Doesn't look the type at all."

Warren merely shrugged. He didn't object to Marge's romancing with both Jack and Kenster. She was obviously having a good time, but he was afraid one of them was going to take her seriously sooner or later. In a way, Warren felt responsible for her. She was a likable youngster, and good at her job. Pretty, too.

He glanced at her, and his mind ran on speculations having nothing to do with the future history of galaxies. With an effort he dragged himself back to the moment.

Marge woke up suddenly, and her first word was, "Darn it, I'll miss the festival, after all!"

She sat up and looked around. "And it was going to be such a bang-up affair. We worked for it a whole month, and I had really a big part in it. I was sure that Bidra was going to get the spot—but was I glad when she didn't!"

"Whoa!" said Warren. "Whoever you were probably did make it. Just Marge McElroy wasn't there. And without your camera, what could you have wanted?"

The girl put her hand to her head a moment. "You know, you're right. I guess I'd rather be here than there anyway. All that dance ritual and star worship rehearsal kept me real busy—or rather it all kept the *other* me—Trince—busy."

"And now you're going to be real busy writing down every little thing that happened to you," Williams said crisply. "Get to that desk, Marge, and start writing before you forget any of it."

Obediently the girl went to the desk. Warren asked one question before she picked up the pen. "Did they have space flight where you were?"

"Oh, yes," she said, starting to write. "They'd had it for centuries. With all those stars in the sky—thousands and thousands of them, and those white nights—space flight was a natural."

She looked up at them a moment. "That sky—I never saw anything like it! It was all blazing, even at night. It made our own stars seem so tiny and far away." She shook her head and bent to her writing.

Warren was anxious to hear the rest of her story; for there seemed something piquant at the thought of this girl, sometimes naive, sometimes with an almost worldly feminine cunning, so definitely the product of her times, wandering far afield in alien worlds with alien histories. She seemed none the worse for it though, and he forebore from interfering with her.

As a matter of fact, he didn't have time to wait for her to finish her script. For he was due in the transferal chamber next. Even before Marge was quite done writing, she was asked to shift to another room to finish, while Warren was prepared for his own transferal.

This time the telescopic trigger was not directed at the original planet Komar but merely in the general astronomic neighborhood. Once a connection had been established, it seemed to become easier and easier for the mental phasing to take place. The social pattern on the micro-cosmic star, its people and the transferee's assumed personality, all left a residue in the memory, as of several months' actual residence there for each short transferal.

Warren sank under the image and the drug. He felt himself blacking out, he felt the same moment of vertigo, then felt himself sitting somewhere. There were voices around him, the sounds of haste and movement, a screeching of small wheels, bumps and bangs as if things were being dropped.

His vision cleared, he looked around. He was sitting at a rough table, a writing instrument in his hand, checking off items on a long sheet of paper. He was tired, and he felt as if he had been sitting there for many hours longer than his usual work day.

About him was a scene of hustling, almost frenetic activity. His seat was at the entrance of a gigantic spacecraft which was in the process of being loaded. But this work was emergency, his mind told him. He recalled that he had been checking off the cargo as it was rushed up, checking and ordering until he was bone-weary. But the work had to be done.

Trucks, rolling on several sets of wheels were being unloaded before the ship's hold. Men, equally weary, haggard in appearance, were unloading, carrying, and wheeling the objects into the ship. They would seem to make little sense, judging by ordinary space cargos—which were generally raw materials, manufactured goods in quantity, objects of art peculiar to special worlds, foods from the home world that would fetch high prices in export, and so forth. But this was no commercial cargo.

There were loads of household goods, hastily tied together with plastic ropes. There were trunks and boxes of clothing—not new clothing, but the everyday clothes of people. There were crated works from the leading museums, the famous paintings, the sterosculp masters, the visi-music machines. There were hasty loads of concentrated foods, the most nutrient in the smallest packages, regardless of flavor. The loading had been going on for eight days, and was nearly over.

Next would be the people. Dimly he heard the noises and shuffling of the crowds that had already arrived and had been waiting patiently. He had paused in the contemplation of this discovery, too tired to rack his new brain for the answers, when a voice spoke next to him:

"Dozing off again, Commander? Better let me finish the job. You go on home, pack your own stuff. get some sleep, and come aboard with your family tomorrow at take-off time. We don't really need you more today."

Warren jerked his nodding head up, looked around. The speaker was his second officer, gnarled Szek. He stared at him a moment, nodded. "You're right," he said. "I can't keep this up. Take the desk."

Warren got up. The other, an old space-hand whose bald Komarian head was speckled from long exposure to cosmic rays, took over the endless task of listing the incoming cargo. Warren, now in the body and mind of Neith Heart-in-hand, commander of the great space cruiser *Formidable* of the Ultra-Komarian Empire's navy, made his way out of the enclosure separating the vast battle craft from the throng of civilians outside. All around him the bustle of loading continued. Once outside the gates, the crowd respectfully made way for him, recognizing him as the man who would be responsible for their safety.

He flew to his home in one of the suburbs in a single-seater rent-o-plane. As he sailed over the nearly deserted city, he looked down on it and was sad, for the city had been a great one and the planet, Morlna, a proud planet, one of the great colonial descendants of ancient Komar. The city itself was seven hundred years old, the planet's colony only eight hundred.

Now it was to vanish.

Warren's mind searched the thoughts of Neith's brain and the story was awe-inspiring. It had been a thousand years after the first landing on another star's planet, and that first starship had returned with half its brave crew missing. But it had been succeeded by others, and the men and women of Komar had forced a toehold on the worlds of other stars; forced, held, and finally conquered them. The sagas of planetary colonies were magnificent; none, he thought, more so than the story of his own world.

There had been troubles and dangers, massacres, and plagues. The first small villages and settlements had survived, spread out, and Morlna had prospered. Now, it was a world that had seen millions of happy citizens. And it was a doomed world. For the sun about which Morlna revolved was about to become a nova. It was about to burst into a ball of atomic fire many times its present size; it would explode within itself.

The heat and fire of the coming nova would utterly destroy all life-forms on Morlna. The surface would be scorched, the atmosphere burned away. But they had had warning, and the entire Empire of twenty-nine planets on twenty stars had united to rescue the people of Morlna.

The space fleet had been sent, the cruisers and battle craft, the explorer vessels, the cargo vessels, the freighters, the passenger liners. For two years all had been busy, carting away people and possessions. Now there was but the cruiser *Formidable*, its interior ripped out to make room for two thousand fleeing passengers and their possessions. They were the last two thousand people of the planet, the last citizens of the great city that had been Neith's home.

Neith arrived home, a spreading, pleasant many-roomed building on the green park that surrounded the city. His wife and two children welcomed him, and he was so tired that he went right to sleep. He awoke in the early dawn, and knew the time had come. He packed his family in the family air scooter, piled in their bags, and turned for a last look. For a long moment Neith and his wife looked at their home, looked at the things they could not take and would never see again save in the tri-D pictures stored among their treasures.

Then they returned to the *Formidable*. The two thousand passengers had almost completely filed in. Inside, Neith saw that his crew, directed by his medical officers and pharmacist ratings, had been putting them under suspension and stacking the unconscious forms in narrow bins like so much cordwood. But this was the practical way; it saved space, it saved food, it prevented disharmony.

He kissed his own wife and children good-by, and they too were taken for suspension. Then he went to the bridge.

There was a delay of two more hours while the last of the cargo was stored, while the ship was checked for space-worthiness. There was a strange silence among the crew—mainly men of Morlna. At the bridge Neith and Szek silently stared at the landscape.

"It looks so calm and peaceful," remarked Neith finally. "You wouldn't know."

The other assented. "But I think already the sun is brighter." Neith looked up, strained his eyes to where the sun was rising in the morning sky. "You may imagine it," he said. "The time is not for a few more hours."

"May I remind you that the astronomers were not so definite. They can only estimate the approximate time, not the exact time. I still think it looks strange," was Szek's rejoinder.

And Warren/Neith looked again, studied it. It looked as if there might be some truth to this observation. It did seem like simply a bright sun on a clear morning, yet perhaps it was a bit brighter. He squinted a moment more, then, turning, pressed the general alarm bell.

At the sound of the gongs throughout the ship, the crew hastened their work. It meant take-off in a few minutes. Hastily they waved the last person inside, bolted and sealed the ports. The second alarm made the ship ready, and at the third, the ship gently rose on its anti-gravitational beams, heading for the skies.

At the bridge Neith and Szek were strained, watching the automatic registers of the ascendancy into the dark of space, and at the same time watching the alarming changes already taking place in the sun. For the great star was already beginning its internal disruption. Its coronal display was several times greater than had ever been seen before; some of the flames now ascending to what Neith mentally supposed must be a million miles. He ordered the utmost acceleration.

The starship leaped forward. Soon the planet Morlna was but a great green-and-blue globe, partly lighted by the flaming sun, and hanging in the blackness of space. Neith could see its main continent, the land mass known as Dau-volna, the land of Dau, in honor of the first master of space. He could see its bays and inlets, its two great rivers, its mountain ranges.

Even as he watched he could see the clouds gathering across the face of the land and seas as the unusual heat of the enlarging sun struck the surface. Now he noticed clouds of black along the green surface and knew them to be forest fires springing up everywhere.

The world fell back, dwindled rapidly as the ship sped outward, away from the sun, away from Morlna's orbit. Even as it sped, he could see the sky of Morlna darkening, turning gray with clouds and smoke. Turning elsewhere he could see the sun that had once been so friendly, glowing bright and white and furious, already had expanded to twice its size, and was still rapidly growing.

He rang for more speed, but they had already reached the maximum so close to a sun. The *Formidable* was accelerating at its top rate. In another few minutes it would be nearly at the speed of light. The speed was barely enough. For the sun's rays were traveling at the full speed of light, and before the ship would get far enough away in space to be safe, the new increased blast of heat would catch them.

There were no other ships in space. The last freighters had left two days before and were safely beyond, on their way to the nearer stars.

The *Formidable* sped on; the sun exploded behind them. Its planets reduced to ashes, its appalling light finally reached out into space and caught up with the speeding starship. Within the ship it was as if the vessel had been struck a blow by a great hand. There was a perceptible jolt. The ship's insulation fought to hold the inner temperature at a bearable point. Inside the air warmed steadily.

Neith fought with the controls, knowing he dare not increase the ship's speed—and, as a matter of fact, any possible increase would be too slight to matter. With despair he knew there was but one course left to him. He must drive on and hope that eventually they would outreach the great circle of incredible heat from the exploding sun.

The heat within the ship grew steadily greater, and various little elements began to show signs of going haywire. One by one the refrigeration mechanisms blew from the strain. The atomic piles were showing evidence of an overload of incoming energy. The cosmic ray drive was swaying off the usual streams due to the impact.

Finally the ship's engines blew altogether. There was a

terrible period of darkness, as all over the ship light and power went out—the atomic piles completely shorted by a flow of energies unparalleled in space history. In darkness and deadness the *Formidable* tore on, its course askew, its cosmic stream diverted.

Neith carried on as best he could, but he finally succumbed under the strain. He felt himself slipping into unconsciousness, a mass of raw skin and dripping perspiration. At last he blacked out. . . .

He came to consciousness he did not know when. The ship was still traveling. He lifted his head from the control board to note that the lights were on, and the board again functioning.

Beside him Szek stirred, then the others. Buzzers began to sound on his board which indicated that all over the ship the crew were returning to their posts.

A hasty check of the ship showed that it was again in action. Apparently the *Formidable* had managed, after all, to elude the outer edges of the nova. And once away from the distortion, the atomic engines reasserted themselves, the cosmic stream took hold again.

Neith/Warren took survey of the ship's position among the stars. For a moment he was nonplused. He rapidly rechecked the course, and there was no doubt of it; the ship had been shifted considerably. Also, it had been moved incredibly faster than its best speed under its own power. And at sometime—there was no telling how long everyone had been unconscious—the *Formidable* had passed its original objective, a new colonial planet of the next star. Now, unbelievably, that star was behind them—a good dozen light years behind them—and he was taking his ship and two thousand sleeping passengers into new and unexplored stellar territory.

While the crew were checking the cargo and the unconscious passengers, Neith and his officers worked out their position. They started to bring the great ship around in a vast circle which would bring it on an orbit through the sector of unknown space and out finally into the circuit of another outpost of the Ultra-Komarian Empire. But it would be a long trip—one of dozens of years by planetary standards—and the crew realized that when they did arrive they would find themselves having long been listed among the dead.

But there was no other possible course. And so Neith set it.

Days and weeks went by, and still the ship plowed on through the unexplored stars, turning steadily to go back to the worlds they knew. Then one day, while Neith was sitting in thought at the bridge, there was an alarm.

The ship's crew was startled. Neith's officers held the opinion that a search ship had come up to them. They strained their eyes for the first glimpse of the other craft, the one which had tripped their area of radar sensitivity. Finally the dot was sighted, and eagerly they watched it grow.

Szek was tense but smiling. "It'll be great to hear news again from the home worlds," he said. "There are a lot of people aboard this ship who had relatives rescued first. They'll be glad to know we're safe."

Neith was staring uneasily at the incoming craft. "I think you've all failed to notice something," he finally remarked quietly. His officers ceased their bantering and listened. "Do you notice where that ship is coming from? How do you suppose it got there?"

They all looked again. Then they became quiet, and two swore softly beneath their breath. The other craft was approaching them in an orbit that did not come from the Komarian worlds which lay far to one side of them. It was coming directly out of another sector of sky, on an orbit that by no possible stretch of the imagination could have originated within the vast boundaries of the Empire.

"What is it?" muttered Szek. "What can it be?"

Neith would not have known, but Warren Alton in his brain did. It was Warren who put the words in Neith's mouth. "It can only be a ship from another star system. From a world that has discovered space flight for itself!"

Warren remembered the last discussion at Enderby's table. There were more than a half-dozen worlds that had discovered and practiced space flight. That had been about fifteen hundred Komar years ago. Those worlds would not have lagged in developing and improving their craft nor their techniques.

Could it be Weidekind's sector? Or Williams's sector? Desperately Warren tried to recall the details of the reports of the other worlds, but they were vague to him. Then he remembered the physical dimensions of the microcosm and it came to him that the oncoming stranger could be from none of the worlds covered by the scientists of Project Microcosm. They were all too remote from this wing of the spiral galaxy.

The newcomer was an unknown. But Neith/Warren was armed with the knowledge that these strangers could not be much different, could scarcely be more backward, or more advanced. So when the oncoming vessel had loomed to a disc of light and the radio began to crackle with the words of a command in a language unknown to all, he did not make the mistake of panicking.

"We should stand and fight," urged Szek and the other officers agreed. "Ram 'em," urged a deck officer. "Blast 'em, with our tail-rocket assembly!" said a gunner.

Neith shook his head. "We have two thousand men and women aboard this ship, and our first duty is to them. I propose to take no action that will jeopardize them. The minds in that ship may be alien to us, but they cannot be stupid, animal-like monsters if they have mastered the same laws of nature that we have."

Now the stranger flashed a light three times, and was

close enough to have its details showing. It was a sharp-nosed craft, undoubtedly foreign in design, and yet clearly a star ship designed for speed, maneuverability, and combat.

Neith ordered a hull light blinked three times, likewise in indication of acknowledgment. The stranger came around, drew up parallel to the *Formidable* and blinked again, drawing slightly ahead. It was plain to all that they were expected to follow it.

Neith matched his great ship's pace to that of the stranger and the two ran on, heading, he determined, for a star glowing ahead of them, whose rays could be seen lighting a family of seven planets. A tiny globe detached itself from the stranger and worked its way across space to the side of the *Formidable*. There was a knock at the particular hull-port where the space-boat came to rest. Neith himself got up to go to meet the strangers, and he felt himself in a curious state of mental exaltation and alarm. This was a moment in history of great significance. He felt drained as he walked to the port, and as he walked he seemed to get dizzy; he felt a moment of vertigo. . . .

Warren, at that instant, recovered consciousness in the transferal chamber at Thunderhook Mountain.

CHAPTER ELEVEN

DURING THE next six weeks the researchers of Thunderhook Mountain found that a great many changes were going on in their mental attitudes. It was a result that they really hadn't anticipated, and was due to the curious time-shifts each man underwent when engaging in transferal.

For what it amounted to was this: In that period, each of the transferees lived a period of six weeks on the planet Earth at the place called Project Microcosm, and their physical bodies aged but forty-two biological days in that time—nothing visible at all. But in the same time, their minds and memories had been stocked with many years of actual day-by-day, minute-by-minute life as inhabitants of a multitude of different worlds. Also these worlds were never alien to those whose minds were phased onto them. For within the brains of people born and raised in these planets of a universe beyond physical touch and control, their home worlds were familiar and natural, and everything upon them was the normal state of society and nature.

Thus each had lived for varying periods of two to ten months as part and parcel of humanoid societies, sharing the family life, the daily problems, the worries, the hopes, the ambitions and the pleasures of these societies, and sharing them as natural members of such social systems, and not as visitors from an alien world. The increased concentration of the staff on these transferals had literally added years crammed with memories and emotional involvements to the characters and psyches of scientists on Thunderhook Mountain.

As a result of this space-time aging, these added experiences in depth, each of those involved had undergone a change in personality. It was shown in a mellowing, an accumulation of wisdom and patience, a deeper insight, a certain unusual emotional maturing in many of these people. Perhaps they were not altogether aware of this themselves, but the non-participating members of the staff noticed it.

Jack and Kenster and the other guard noticed it. Whereas before they had made an adjustment to the learned men they guarded, they found that they had to readjust constantly. This in particular was the case with Marge McElroy. As she had returned again and again to the world in the hub of the microcosm she had gained exactly that worldly wisdom that her city childhood had failed to give her. In her mind she had memories of motherhood, of love given, of love denied, of life devoted to ideals, of life devoted to religion. She was as a result, in that small space of six weeks, a far more mature and enriched person. Still a sweet and smiling young girl, she looked upon the guards now for what they were—husky strong men of not much education, perception nor native intelligence. For she had known men of quality and women of forebearance, and that knowledge had done her well. She was in some ways not clear as to her relationship with the men about her; she recognized a lack in herself, yet knew also that never again could she be the same rather superficial and at times self-centered girl.

Jack Quern had managed to kiss her a few times during the first four weeks, but soon he sensed in her an aloofness, a growing disinterest in this childish play of cheap romancing. He was angered by it, attributed it to some other man— probably one of the scientific staff—cutting in. He wasn't sure who it was, but he began to keep an eye on her to spot the egghead who had cut him out.

As for Marge herself, she gave only part of her time to work on the endless photographic records kept by Steiner and Marco. She was by no means an ideal reporter, but her records of the rise and historical changes in the world where she had spent mental years—were of interest. For one, it was a world which had developed along less materialistic lines than most. Possibly due to its position in the middle of the greatest point of star concentration, the inhabitants had acquired a fixation on the glory of their heavens—they had evolved a rather unique astrological theocracy, given over to elaborate ritual, dance, and vast musical concepts.

In the course of the rising evolution of the microcosmic civilizations, this world, too, had been visited by the space fliers from other planets, and finally had become integrated into the vast network of linked intelligences.

For that had proved to be the course of intelligence in that microcosm. It was Enderby's view that it would also prove the inevitable course of life in the future of our own universe. Whether that were so or not, it was certainly shown to be a route that all had to traverse within the hundred thousand planets of the man-made universe.

Even as the Ultra-Komarian Empire had colonized and created a federation of planets in its own sector, so had other space-traveling worlds in their sectors. In time these sectors began to overlap—civilization met civilization. Starship met starship; not always in as spectacular a fashion as that which had followed the nova of Morlna's star, but somehow in some fashion, it had to happen.

These meetings were sometimes peaceful, as had been the aftermath of the Morlna episode. Warren had read the full account of this momentous meeting during a transferal a thousand years later when he had deliberately looked it up. The account was found in a tri-D transcription taken from the yellowing and crumbling volumes in the Hall of Archives in the great university at Komar. The librarians had looked in surprise at the young physics student—which was Warren during that transfer—who had insisted with youthful intensity on that particular antique book.

But sometimes the meetings of the interplanetary civilizations were more militant.

There were star empires that had come to blows at first meeting, quarreling over possession of a planet or over some slight. These empires had clashed in vicious battles of hurtling spacecraft in the empty outer reaches, with sneak raids on undefended worlds.

But even those clashes had ceased as more and more planetary combinations took to the field. Finally the day had come when empires combined to form mightier confederations. And these confederations in turn, across a few thousand more years, combined to make sector centers.

There was the memorable affair on which Warren had finished reporting as they sat around the great table on Thunderhook Mountain. It had been Warren's most recent transferal, and his story had held them all spellbound, even though they had been used to wonders and marvels.

For Warren had been a participant at the Galactic Congress which had voted to combine the six great sector federations into one single all-embrasive League of Planets.

The Congress had met in the great city of Dau, capital of the Federation of the Southwest, and Warren had been one of that federation's sixty-two delegates, as a representative of three worlds.

He described to them the vast hall—really several great halls linked together with tri-D telecommunications which gave each hall the appearance of being one with all the others. He described the various types of beings present at that meeting—human in all general appearance, but exotically different in various ways. The crested feather-skulls from one planet, the dwarfmen of another, the eight-footers from one world, and the odd-hued skins and colorful ceremonial dress of a hundred different planets. Most had two eyes, a few had four, one planet group had a single eye centered in their foreheads.

They had voted Dau the capital of their galaxy; this city, named after perhaps a mythical forerunner of space flight, one of the oldest planetary cities.

As he spoke, Williams nodded for he had missed that gathering only by a century, but it had been talked of in his day. Weidekind was fascinated, for he was going off to transferal next and would see the one-galaxy system in operation in its earliest years. Enderby himself had made a number of transfers, and so of course had the others, save Steiner and Marco. But these two were old enough to have acquired wisdom through their own years, and they left the wandering to the younger men.

Marge sat at the table, sitting gravely silent, listening with interest. But she sat more erectly, she was subtly different, and Warren was vastly intrigued by her. Lately, several times they had conversed and he found that the latent attraction which had first simply amused him, was now becoming a growing emotional thing. He felt that he wanted to see her, wanted to talk and walk with her. Even as he was recounting the discussions and the differences that had occupied the Galactic Congress, his mind turned on how he could get to chat with Marge that evening.

The problem of combining the federations was no easy one. Many of its elements had been solved during the earlier centuries, but working on the whole galaxy was a different and more complex matter. With a galaxy that was a universe, starship voyages took periods of time which were for years out of touch with their home-worlds. Within the starships, no voyage was too intolerable. The problem was not that; the hot problem was to keep contact between worlds without too much loss of time.

In essence, the solution had been found in quite the same way as the men of Thunderhook had transfered their minds. Not in mind-power, but in the deliberate creation of blocks of matter so exactly balanced that they vibrated in precise sympathy with each other. For such a block would vibrate simultaneously with its phased companion, regardless of whether a galaxy separated the two units. As a result of this, it had been possible to set up whole communication systems for the exchange of messages and vision across a hundred thousand worlds simultaneously.

So this congress had another unique quality, a symbolic one. It was a meeting of physical beings which might never occur again. There was no actual need for the delegates to see each other. They could have communicated easily without taking the time and inconvenience of cosmic trips. They could have stayed in their home worlds and talked to each other.

But for the sake of the moment, as a means of impressing forever the unity of the galaxy, this meeting had been decided. In the future, in the city of Dau, there would be the sympathetic tuners of all the worlds, and it would act as the central station for all interchanges.

So this meeting was the first physical gathering, and would be the last such of the microcosm. It was Warren's glory to have been there.

After his report had been given and discussed, the meeting broke up. There had been a brief discussion of the spy problem—there had been evidence of other attempts to copy the data, but they had been thwarted. Enderby nevertheless warned everyone that it could be expected that these efforts would continue until the spy had achieved success, or been exposed. He urged caution. "We are," he had said, "now in possession of the scientific secrets that mankind here is not due to discover for the next twenty thousand years. We must take care in our guardianship of these secrets; very great care."

Later that day, when most of the men had left the supper table for a quiet game of cards, or to read and smoke, Warren went out for a stroll.

It was deep in the summer. The sky was not entirely dark, the horizon was glowing violet from the last moments of twilight. A single spot of white indicated the planet Venus, the Evening Star, pioneering the celestial procession of oncoming night. There was the smell of pine in the air, the dampness of the encircling forested mountainsides, the twilight twittering of birds, and the first sounds of the crickets.

Warren walked slowly over the grass in the cleared area outside the group of buildings that composed Project Microcosm. There was a rise of hill beyond on which he had sometimes ascended in past evenings to stand quietly and smoke a pipe, while watching the stars come out. It was a period of meditation.

He was a different man from the one he had been the day he drove upstate on this assignment. In his mind were memories of other beings' lives. He recalled other moments, standing on alien countrysides, meditating on other landscapes, looking at other skies. He remembered the rest periods on the Ice Moon, shivering in his space suit and looking into the airless black void. He recalled a vacation with his wife in the seashore of Morlna, and her laughter and the sound of the flying fish. He remembered other times and other worlds. And they were all real, all poignant.

Yet this was his own world, this universe his. The other, though its spaces were vast, was yet finite. Compared to this infinite universe of the Milky Way and its attendant galaxies and meta-galaxies, it was a mere bubble—a space-time bubble, with definite boundaries on all sides. These boundaries were charted; the League of Planets had arrived at such knowledge—and beyond them there would be nothing for the inhabitants. But our own universe was infinite, so far as man could determine. Bursting into existence somehow, it seemed to go on forever, spreading out, its parts rushing away steadily—one theory holding that new parts were constantly being spawned. This was infinity. Could it be, then, that for world humanity there were no limits?

It was growing darker as he reached the top of the little hill. Behind him were the lights of the main lodge and the few lights from the other buildings. All around were the dark shadows of the mountain tops, and overhead was the arch of the sky, with here and there a few stars beginning to show up through the darkening blue.

He noticed that there was someone else on the hill, a figure seated in the grass, sitting quietly. "Hello," he ventured, "who's there?"

The figure looked at him. He saw a glimpse of face and the darker outline of a mass of hair. "It's I," said Marge's voice. "Just came up here to look at the sky and think."

"Me too," he answered. "Mind if I join you?" He squatted down on the grass near her and for a while they were both silent, watching the sky darken to blackness and the stars begin to appear.

After a while they could see the wide band of the Milky Way stretching across the heavens and the twinkling lights of myriad stars. "It's a wonderful sight, isn't it?" he asked.

She was silent for a while longer. "Yes," she finally said. "It's wonderful. It isn't like the sky where I have been. That's wonderful too, but in a different way. That sky, so filled with big white stars, is more awesome. It tends to overpower you, to bear down on you weightily. This sky is easier, yet so much more intense. Somehow it seems to get into you, to get at your soul with its suggestion of depth and space, its feel of immortality."

He nodded and puffed at his pipe.

After a long silence, she went on, speaking softly as if to herself. "I feel humble before all this, yet I also feel that I ought to be singing. I feel a connection with everything, with the trees and the grass, with the insects and the wind and the very rocks around me. Gazing into our sky gives me a deep harmony with existence."

Warren gazed into the heavens meditatively. He nodded. "You've changed, Marge," he said. "Do you know that? So, I guess, have I. This business has changed us all. But I think it has done wonders for you, most of all. You don't seem the same kid that came out here only a few months ago."

Marge drew in her breath, gave him a quick glance in the darkness. "I—I don't know what you mean," she said. "Though I hope it's meant as a compliment."

His smile was concealed by the darkness. She was a different girl; there was something about her that made him feel warm and relaxed.

They sat there for another half hour, saying little but finding a quiet contentment under the stars. Then they got up and walked slowly back through the dark starlit night to the lodge. He said good-by to her when she went upstairs, and walked briefly back to the records hall to see if all was in order. This was a nightly recheck that he had undertaken as part of the general security measures.

On his way between the buildings, a dark figure came up to him, blocked him. "Alton!" said the other, and he recognized the voice of the guard, Jack Quern.

He started to move around him, but Jack's hand came out and grabbed his arm. "Listen here, Alton. I don't like you moving in on my girl. I been takin' the kid around, and I ain't the kind of guy to let some smart-aleck cut me out. Lay off, see. Or else!"

A flash of anger surged through Warren. "Or else—what?"

"Or else this!" came the reply. But Warren ducked before Quern's fist could land. He twisted agilely, and swung a hard-fisted right. For a few seconds there was a scuffle. Quern was a good street fighter, but in Warren he was dealing with a man who had learned the tricks of combat in the armed service. Warren was not hurt, but hoped he'd landed a few on the guard.

They broke clear and harsh words were spoken. But Warren warned him coolly that Marge was "nobody's girl" and whom she saw was strictly her own business.

As he left the angry guard, Warren debated with himself as to his own emotions in regard to the girl. He suspected he knew. He'd run into a lot of young ladies who thought a well-known foreign correspondent was a good catch, yet somehow none of them had struck an answering spark. But on a hillside overlooking the strangest and vastest project in scientific history, that spark had been struck. . . .

CHAPTER TWELVE

SAVE FOR ONCE or twice, Leopold Steiner had not been a regular participant in the transferal program. But at the round table session that took place a week later, he was the center of attraction. For what he had to say was of the utmost importance.

He began the meeting by discussing briefly the origin of their man-made universe in a single giant protoatom of hydrogen, standing outside our own space and time. He went on to describe the explosion of this atom, and how its component parts spread outward, first as the thinnest of gases, then began to draw together into cosmic dust, and this in turn into the various elements and finally the stars and planets of a single galactic cluster.

"This galaxy has been expanding still, enlarging by the lasting momentum of the original explosion, even as our own universe is also expanding. But whereas we are now certain that our universe is infinite and that it is also probable that new matter is coming into existence all the time, we also know that such is not the case with our experiment. We, after all, created it, even if we cannot control it afterward. We also know that we ourselves have established its limits.

"It is limited by the encysting forces of our space-time continuum, a segment of which has been torn apart to allow it to exist, but which is also governed by space-time resistance. It is further checked by the application of atomic power generated here at our own plant. This augments the natural resistance of our own universe and which, working together, is capable of equaling the total energy of the micro-universe itself.

"Thus the continuous expansion of our microcosm is definitely limited. I must now tell you that its outward expansion has reached its limits; that it has stopped expanding; and that it is beginning to contract."

He paused, looked around to see if all were following him. Warren was sitting tilted back in his chair, listening calmly. From what he gathered, the end of the experiment was approaching. The others seemed a little disturbed. Marge, however, was leaning forward, her face tense.

"Do you mean that the microcosm is facing its end?" she asked Steiner.

The world-famous physicist looked at her, shrugged. "Not any more immediately than we had supposed. It may take another two or three years to end. It will be interesting to know how. And, of course, we must wait until it happens."

Marge shook her head impatiently. "Yes, I understand that it may take time for it all to end. But I was thinking of the planets, and more especially of the life on them. Will this affect them soon, and if so, how?"

Steiner rubbed his chin. "I suppose it will affect them. That is an interesting speculation, yes. But how, and to just what degree, we don't know yet. He paused a moment.

"You see," he started, "we have been measuring the drift of the micro-universe stars and the movement of the galaxy and its clusters. We have now seen that the outermost fringes, having reached the outer borders of the micro-universe, find themselves distorted in space. They are subject to a dimensional twisting which turns them back—forces them to rebound, if you will. They expend their outward energy, start to fall slowly back toward the center of the universal sphere. This process began slowly, but we now see it full swing.

"As the stars and their attendant planets begin to move back toward the common center, they will begin to make for a concentration of gases and material at the hub. Before this, there had been an attenuation of this concentration, which permitted the growth of life, among other things. Now a reverse of the process will occur. As the stars fall back and concentrate they will tend to accumulate heat. They will seem to return to a more primitive condition. Eventually we may suppose they will form a concentrated mass of energy and matter at the very center—the very reconstitution of the primitive atom.

"As for the planets—which you know, from a strictly astrophysical viewpoint, are the least significant of cosmic materials—they will probably become untenable to life as soon as this process is generally under way. I would say they might have another few million years before the last and most rugged forms of bacterial life are wiped out. Much sooner, of course, for the more highly organized forms of life. Maybe your League of Planets could last a hundred thousand more years before these civilizations become hopelessly disrupted in the accumulating heat and stellar dust."

He passed around photos indicating the shifts that had taken place.

Warren was now disturbed. "I gather from what you say that we shall now start to witness the end of a universe, the doom of many civilizations and those who live within them. Then is there no hope for those people?"

Weidekind answered him. "How could there be? We all know that every world must eventually end. It will be very interesting to see how the individual inhabitants meet it."

"A depressing thought," said Enderby. "Nonetheless this microcosm has benefited our own world, and so in that way you could say that the inhabitants lived on."

Marge was pale. She said in a horrified tone, "And is that to be the be-all and end-all of those wonderful peoples?

The millions and millions of men and women who strived and hoped and suffered to make better homes for themselves, and for each other? Must all their efforts and sacrifices end in heat and slow death, choke out in blankets of cosmic dust, to have their proud cities and constructions and bold, generous plans for the future all back into flames and vanish forever?"

The others, sobered, looked at her. "I'm afraid there's no hope," said Steiner. "Isn't that the ultimate end of all men? You have heard the Biblical saying, 'Dust thou art to dust returneth.' Do you think the death of all men greater than the death of one single man?"

Marge shook her head, vastly disturbed. "I cannot believe it. One man's death is but a single mortal incident—only a part of a much greater whole. The whole, the society, the entire species, was not meant to be destroyed. Men die so that their fellow-men may live. But not all to die."

Enderby broke in. "This will not help. We were privileged to witness the birth of a universe, now we must, perforce, witness its death. Perhaps it was not meant for us to witness these things, we who are mortal. But now that we have embarked on this, we must see the end as well as the beginning."

After that, the relation of the various transferals was something of an anticlimax. Interesting as they might have been at another time, the knowledge of forthcoming doom colored everything. But one thing was clear—so far, apparently, the inhabitants of the microcosm had not discovered for themselves the total end. What was apparent from outside observation was not so easily detected from within.

The microcosm was undergoing the most Utopian era of its existence. Throughout the worlds the pains and agonies of social evolution had terminated in the achievement of world-wide mastery of science and natural laws. Abundance was the rule, and that which one world lacked, it obtained fairly from others. Yet the inhabitants did not lack for interest and work. A multitude of philosophical discussions occupied the best minds, and sports had arisen to a complexity and diversity startling to contemplate. All the arts were reaching heights never before dreamed of—and though little of this could be brought back to the Mountain laboratories in their full depth and complexity, the transferees still managed to amass such records as would keep the minds and artists of Earth busy for centuries to come.

After the meeting broke up and while Warren was preparing to retire, he happened to overhear part of a conversation between Enderby and Stanhope. The photographic expert and chief of their records hall was worried. He had been seeing figures moving around the distant woods. He said he suspected prowlers.

"You think men are camping in the woods near here?" asked Enderby quietly.

Stanhope nodded. "I never see them come into plain sight, but it's as if we were being watched."

Enderby nodded. "Don't mention this to anyone. As a matter of fact, I'm glad to hear of it. As it happens, I have requested additional watchers and what you say confirms my request. Ever since those attempts on the records, I've asked for increased vigilance. I'm sure there's a stake-out being made here to protect us. But say nothing about it. There's someone among us who is not all he pretends to be—just which man I'm still not sure—but until we ferret him out, keep quiet."

Stanhope and Enderby moved out of Warren's hearing. The reporter went up to his room, deep in thought.

The following afternoon, after three others had made transferals, came Warren's turn next. He occupied a special role among the investigators, for it turned out to be his sector that held the central exchange bureau of the League of

Planets. Such was the role of the City of Dau, a Komarian planetary metropolis.

After the transfer, his first impression was of bubbles, hundreds of gorgeous multi-colored bubbles floating gently beneath a blue sky. He was standing somewhere watching bubbles. As he stood, the scene seemed to rock gently and the bubbles seemed to shift and move softly about.

He blinked his eyes, looked hard. Yes, they were bubbles, and they were buildings too. Then the Komarian brain his mind usurped began to supply the answers. Mentally he oriented himself against the change.

This was Dau—but it was a Dau quite changed from the city he'd visited on the great day of the founding of the League. This was Dau twelve thousand years later; a city changed beyond compare. A city having nothing in common save a very ancient name, whose origin was lost in antiquity.

It was a city of great bubbles, bubbles of plastic force, blown permanently and enclosing the living quarters of the city's populace. These bubbles, moving above the surface at the desire of their occupants, were single homes or compound dwellings, as desired. Within them people lived and slept and did their work or pursued their individual interests. The landscape about the city had been returned to natural beauty. Great meadows, flower gardens of delightful color, mountains hewed out for deliberate scenic effect and even several carefully controlled volcanoes, gave richness to the scene. The city occupied the planet, and its homes might be anywhere; over a rolling ocean, in a deliberately planned jungle, or in a beautiful parkland.

The man whose body Warren occupied, whose name is not easily transcribed in an Earthly tongue, turned from gazing out the window. There were rooms in his bubble-home, and they were chambers in keeping with the world outside. Chairs floated gently above the floors; colorful pictures shimmered and moved against the walls, and many devices, unknown to Terra, conveyed pleasure to mind and eye and ear. This was also a work chamber, for it was the duty of the city-world of Dau to act as the records hall and exchange bureau of all the worlds in their universe.

The family in each bubble-home had a connection with certain worlds, and they interchanged and co-ordinated news, scientific discoveries and speculative theories. The communicators were crystalline globes which hung suspended in certain rooms. These were phased in with other such globe-communicators in Dau, and other inhabited planets of the micro-universe. Within them could be seen and heard whatever was visible in the other corresponding globe.

So Warren went back to his work that day, and he watched within the globes the faces of other beings on other worlds and transcribed by sub-atomic memory banks all that was of importance. These memory banks in turn correlated all that was new from everywhere on Dau, sorted it out in vast central storage centers, booked it, catalogued it, cross-filed it.

He exchanged greetings with several of his friends, heard bits of news, filed reports on sports of distant worlds of whose very nature he was ignorant, recorded the latest of arguments on religions and philosophies, with which he had little concern, heeded what intrigued him, placed bets on certain events in an arena of a distant planet that happened momentarily to amuse him.

In that way he spent his day. In his rest period he ate, had a few drinks, talked with companions, saw a female friend and otherwise had an average uneventful day.

Several weeks went by in this languid yet ever full fashion. Warren was caught up in the endless variety of marvels. There was no compulsory work, yet there was so much of fascination in the universe-wide civilization that most of the citizens of Dau actually overworked, but were not conscious of it.

Then one evening as his bubble-home cruised amid the storm clouds of a storm area, while below the trees were lashed by the gales of the controlled weather station, he monitored a discussion of the elections among strange antlike beings of a not fully civilized world, there was a general news alarm. There had not been one for many years. At first he did not know what it was. His communicator globe had suddenly gone black, then cleared to flash red three times in succession.

That was a signal for a universe-wide news story. This would only happen for news that affected everyone—and what sort of story could break like that?

The globe cleared. There was momentary confusion as several channels seemed to fight for space. Then a face emerged briefly. The age-lined features of a well-known astrophysicist. "I break in, friends, to bring you the announcement of a phophecy, and a confirmation. I bring you the recast of the prophecy, made by the Oracle of the White Star two hundred years ago."

His face faded and there came into view a strange face. It was a woman's face, but a curious one, quite unlike the Komarian standards of beauty. She was pale of skin and her head was swathed in a white scarf with a diamond emblem in the form of a star pinned to it. Her brow came down and out in a wide slope, culminating in unexpectedly beetling eyebrows of black. Beneath these brows, sunk very deep in her head, as if hidden from the light, protected by these monstrous crags of brows, were her eyes, dark and deep and shining. Below this beetling brow and probing eyes, her face seemed to taper down quickly. A sharp thin nose, very tiny lips and a tiny chin completed the unusual face.

The effect was eerie, but not surprising to the man of Dau. Those were the features of a race typical to regions of

The Great Glare—worlds circling several suns, or worlds in intense star clusters. But this particular face was familiar.

The woman spoke. She had a ritualistic way of speaking; she seemed to chant her words, but her voice had a haunting quality. And she spoke of coming doom.

She said the universe had reached its outermost expansion; the stars were going to fall back to their original source. She said the end of the worlds was coming, and that all should prepare for it. She said that preparations should be started, for though thousands of years still lay before mankind, there should be no time lost.

Then the face faded. There was a moment of brief silence, then the astrophysicist came in again.

"We have been investigating this prophecy for two hundred years. We are now ready to state our findings. The Oracle is correct. Our measurements have confirmed that our galaxy has ceased its outward motion, that the outer-most fringes of our known stars are beginning to retract, that they have reversed their motion. The red shift of the farthest stars has become a violet one. The universe is beginning to collapse.

"What this means is that the Oracle, through a wisdom peculiar to her office, has spoken truthfully. I return you now to the Oracle of the White Star."

Again the globe cleared and again the face of a white-scarved woman appeared. Yet she was not quite the same woman. She was a person of the same race, of the same oddity of feature, yet a different individual. Nonetheless this person spoke again, affirming the coming doom, urging all to take discussion as to ways and means of saving the lives of all the universe.

The globe faded out. Warren stepped back, sank down into a chair that swooped down to catch him automatically. He stared at the globe. Other faces were now appearing in it, filled with excitement. Talk was beginning to spread.

Warren's mind probed for knowledge of this Oracle. A strange person, how was it she was the first to know of the change in the universe?

Memory came back. The man whose body Warren occupied had seen her several times before, but had paid her little heed. She was an enigma, but one in a galaxy full of enigmas, so that she in particular had never troubled him.

She was regarded on her world as an "eternal" being, yet it could be plainly seen that she was not always the same person; the Oracle of the White Star was a title, yet more than a title. It was apparently a succession of women who, on achieving the title at the death of their predecessor, also seemed to achieve the memories, mentality and personality of the previous Oracle. This strange succession had been going on several thousand years, until the Oracle of the White Star had achieved galaxy-wide fame as a person of more accumulated knowledge than any living being.

She generally spoke in parables and allegories, but she was known on occasion to come forth with some illuminating fact of invention and science which accurately added to the store of universal civilization. She was not easily approachable, answered no questions about herself, and would indulge in personal prophecy on minor occasions.

This then was her discovery. She had known first of the doom, then science confirmed it. She was wise, of that there was no doubt, but to Warren it was doubly curious.

Could a person who somehow had been passed the spark of consciousness that had been steadily burning for thousands of years, be able to tap sources of cosmic knowledge denied to the most learned scientists?

But speculation of this was set aside in the rush of opinions and ideas that flooded the micro-worlds during the remainder of Warren's stay. It was about a year afterward that he blanked out, to find himself again on Thunderhook Mountain. . . .

The reports of all the transferees to come after him confirmed the story. The table reports that night were strangely similar. Through the next two hundred years the discussion was going on. The mental registry on Dau was sorting and threshing out millions of suggestions, each being tested and analyzed. By the last report no practical outcome had been arrived at.

Warren looked at the microcosm itself in the main dome that evening. It appeared changed from the first time he and Marge had seen it. It seemed to have tightened up just slightly, to show signs of curling at the edges. The change was going on.

Early the next morning Warren transferred again. He was back in Dau City once more, again one of its busy citizens working the cross-index of all the collective knowledge of ten thousand worlds.

Six hundred years had passed since the revelation of doom. A number of philosophies had come to the fore. One was a faith of doom. It preached resignation and a concentration on beauty and meditation. This had its converts.

Another was a wild scheme for hollowing out worlds, sealing them up against all cosmic radiance, and dwelling within these worlds for a million years longer than otherwise would be the case. There were many who favored this idea but the physicists scoffed at it. It would, they said, prove impractical and the psychologists said that it would prove to be mental suicide, the immolation of whole worlds.

Then, there was a philosophy of suicide itself. This held that a date be set, ten thousand years in the future, at which time in a mass celebration, all the planets should incinerate themselves in atomic fire. Go out with a blaze of glory.

There was also a group who said a way should be found to break the barriers of time and space—to break through from one universe to another. Warren found that spearheading this viewpoint was the current Oracle of the White Star, and she was gathering support steadily from the leading minds of the galaxy.

The idea of tearing aside the fabric of the very universe itself was a new one. It was the thought that creation was infinite, and that though their own universe seemed to be finite, measurable, and definitely bounded, still this could not be. The intelligent mind could not conceive of an end to itself, nor of an end to existence. If the universe was finite, what was outside it?

A theological concept, yet one which no amount of materialist thinking can ever answer. The mind is simply not constructed to conceive of its own end. On this point the Oracle was hammering away, and she was gaining supporters.

Throughout his seven months' stay in the microcosm during his transferal this debate raged. Even before Warren phased out to return to Project Microcosm and his own body it was apparent that the Oracle's views were going to be tried.

Those who favored resignation would not oppose the others. Those who planned to burrow into their worlds were perfectly free to start digging. The suiciders agreed to hold off until the others had had their trial.

The League of Planets gathered itself for the last great fight. Its millions of minds were working on the problem of breaking through the universal structure itself.

The problem was fantastic in its size. It was apparent from the start that virtually nothing could break the time-space structure of a universe save the application of force equal to or greater than the universe itself. To solve this poser, the minds of a galaxy set to work.

Warren explained all this to the researchers at that evening's council table. But the heads of all who were trained in science shook decisively. Steiner, Marco, Enderby, Weidekind, and the others united in their agreement. The microcosm could not be broken by those within it. All the power at their command could not possibly equal the total sum of the microcosm itself.

"Besides," said Steiner, "we are adding power to its boundaries from our own atomic pile here on Thunderhook. Even if they could concentrate a large fraction of their suns' energies upon one small sector, the constant application of our magnetic brakes, powered by sources outside their universe, will counter anything they could do."

"But," said Weidekind brightly, "it will be grand to watch. A fitting climax. It should make a good story in your history of this experiment, Warren."

Warren looked around. None of the scientists, despite their own deep associations with the microcosm, seemed particularly depressed. They all retained that damnable impersonal look of the dedicated objective observer. But there was one other face besides his own, that reflected deep concern and despair. It was Marge's.

CHAPTER THIRTEEN

A TENSION gripped the project on Thunderhook Mountain during the next week which was quite as deep in its own way as the tension that was gripping the worlds of the microcosm during their next three thousand years. It was to be expected that those who transfered to the worlds of the man-made universe would be affected by the prevailing mood.

A man does not spend the better part of a year in the

company of a society feverish with the knowledge of forthcoming doom and then return for a day in normal Earth company without the hangover of this mental attitude. Yet there was perhaps something to justify the growing concern on Thunderhook itself.

The reports of strangers having been seen in the surrounding woods were confirmed, and it was now known that their guards had been augmented by some sort of outer ring—a group of hired watchmen spaced out along the mountain sides. The scientists were aware that the data within their records was extremely powerful; in the wrong hands it could mean ruin to the world. Not merely space flight, but star flight; the secrets of tapping cosmic energy, the secrets of harnessing sun power direct, the architectural plans for redesigning planets, blueprints for manipulating gravity and the forces beyond gravity—all these were the products of the microcosm experiment. And now that that microcosmic civilization was about to expire, it seemed that there would be no further scientific revelations.

Plainly, as Enderby explained to Warren one time, this is the time for their hidden spy to make his strike and run. Hence the guards, hence the tension.

Besides, there was the question as to what would happen when the united worlds of the microcosm made their effort to break out of the bounds of their own universe. Notwithstanding the certainty that it could not succeed, the intimate knowledge of the attack made things vibrate.

The Oracle of the White Star's voice could be heard on all occasions during transferals, urging haste, firmly asserting that they would succeed, challenging all the facts and figures put forward by the mathematical and physical theorists of a thousand worlds. "Facts and figures may play you false. We have nothing to lose. We will break through," her voice would repeat, and echo and re-echo from every room on every world in a whole universe.

We will try, but the facts are against us. A part can never be greater than the whole. The most we can muster will be but a fraction of our universe's content—and that fraction can never cancel the mass of the whole. Where is your proof that there is another universe? Show us evidence, show us the slightest shred of proof of this existence that is outside of existence."

Still the Oracle held up this one flame of hope—the hope that is beyond logic—"It is there. We must gather our energies and strike out. Believe in me and fight!"

And on Thunderhook at meals and in discussions, the voice of the Oracle would be repeated by the transferees and the voices of Steiner and Marco and Enderby would dissent. "Where is the evidence they can have of an existence outside of their own?" There can be no contact between universes having different time-space continuums. A part can never be greater than the whole.

"And even if they bring the entire energy-mass of the entire microcosm against the barriers of our space, we can add powers that will forever overbalance them."

But the repetition of the Oracle had a hypnotic effect. Even those who did not believe, such as Weidekind and Hyatt, Rendell and Williams, found themselves more and more agitated and more and more irritated. Tempers were getting touchy.

"It is a hard thing to be in two camps at once," said Warren to Marge one morning. "It is like trying to root for both sides at once, and trying to fight for both sides at once."

The girl looked at him. That week she seemed flushed, gripped by tension. "But I cannot help feeling that Steiner and the others are wrong. The scientific knowledge of microcosm savants are so much more advanced than theirs . . . and the microcosm people are going ahead with their plans."

She spoke softly, but Warren knew that she was hoping for the success of the break-out project. Like a woman, she had identified herself with those crying for help, and no logic would sway her new loyalty. He answered by reminding her that even those other brains, trained in advanced physics beyond that of Steiner, did not truly believe in the breakthrough. All were being swayed by a mere will to believe, carried by the chanting hypnotic voice of a mystic.

Marge glanced at him, but held her tongue. And Warren went to his transferal. He slid into the troubled world of Dau City, two thousand years after the pronouncement of doom.

Gone were the bubbles, gone the landscaping. Every energy media of the world—and it was the same on all worlds—was going into the creation of the world-ship. This was the vessel that would carry the seeds of the Komarian people on the break-through attempt. The planet was now seamed and pitted, where vast veins of metals had been gouged out and used in the construction of the ship. The fields had become jungles and beasts ranged the storm-swept nights. In some spots untamed volcanoes raged, the by-product of the ruthless methods used in tearing apart the planet to produce what they needed.

The bubble houses, cut in half into domes, squatted on the polar plateaus, clustering into great colorless cities of toil and hysteria. Those who were working on the world-ship were dedicated men, raised from childhood in an atmosphere of grim urgency, finding their happiness only in the completion of another segment of the world-ship. And others, those who had chosen a different philosophy, were apart from the ship workers.

In their cities hysteria reigned. There was a constant rise and fall of new cults and weird philosophies. There was a mood among many of "*après nous le deluge*" and these made pleasure their sole aim of life. Others devoted themselves to a constant re-examination of their souls.

Between these various viewpoints there was not much harmony. The peace was established mainly by the veritable exclusive fanaticism of each philosophy.

The world-ship was a fantastic thing. Warren worked on it for seven months during that period. It was a spaceship whose length was over a thousand miles, whose widths and diameters were similarly great, which would carry, stacked like cordwood, a quarter of the population of the globe, which would carry in its cargo chambers the entire contents of the greatest museums, libraries, and record halls. It would be driven by consuming the entire energies of mighty suns— its drive the sub-cosmic beams that grasped the basic tensions of the universe itself and burning up entire suns in mighty controlled nova-flashes, hurling itself forward in an unstoppable drive.

The ship would be completed in another thousand years, and on other worlds similar ships were being constructed. When all were ready, they would gather together in one mighty fleet, cannibalize in their drive a thousand mighty suns, and burst together at the farthest point of the universe— an area lacking in stars and where the pull of gravity of the galactic mass would be at its lowest. It was the opinion of the saner scientists that the net result would see the ships tearing along a giant curve, eventually exhaust their drive, and at last find themselves merely turned around the four-dimensional bounds of their universe and still within it.

Other scientists said the result would be total incineration of the ships, sun-drive and all, in a giant explosion.

And the Oracle's voice was always heard, repeated by record every day. She was predicting victory, promising another and greater universe beyond their dying one.

After months of work amid the beams and structures of the Komarian world-ship, the reiterated prophecy of the Oracle rang in Warren's ears like a steady background chant. He found that the mind he occupied believed it, accepted it on faith, and did not allow it to occupy the same thought processes involved in his exact engineering calculations. One was faith, the other mechanics.

So the week went on. Each transferee saw the work go on, each came back with his mind ringing with the sounds of massive construction and vibrating with the insistence of the Oracle's voice. At Thunderhook, the conference table was like a council of war, as Enderby tried to work out from the reports the exact moment the breakthrough would be attempted.

Coupled with this was the feeling of trouble in the hills. Stanhope reported an attempt that had been made to break into the records hall in the middle of the week. The door had been jimmied, the hall had been entered. But an alarm that had been installed was tripped and the intruder had fled.

Finally it was clear that the time had come for the breakthrough attempt of the microcosmic worlds. On Warren's last trip, Friday afternoon, the Komarian ship was complete and being loaded. It hung in the sky of the planet like a new satellite, a strange glistening silver satellite. Steadily going to it were the men, women and children who had elected to take the chance. Streams of spaceship ferries were rising up, loading and returning. In the cities, among the non-believers, a regular bacchanalia was going on. The planet would be theirs and they were preparing to have their way.

Warren brought back the date the attempt would be made. His date, and those returned by others in transferal that Friday, confirmed each other. The attempt would be made that very evening, sometime about eleven o'clock at night, Thunderhook time.

Enderby alerted the staff. Warren and Marge, after supper, went up to the great dome to take a look at the microcosm.

Steiner came on duty with them, relieving Marco. The three stood on the narrow balcony that ran round the inside of the great dome and stared at the pulsing sphere of the mighty microcosm. Outside of the slight astronomical changes due to the passage of time, no one could detect the moment of crisis that gripped the planets within that universe. Its spiral galaxy seemed tighter, but its stars still glowed and its awesome interior was still a peep into a universe outside our own space and time.

They stood there in silence for quite a while. The humming of the magnetic beams that held the micro-universe in check filled the dome. Marge stirred by Warren's side, saying, "It seems ages since we came to this place."

Warren nodded. "It has been ages, truly. Who would have thought that chasing down a crazy story about upstate mirages would have led to our taking part in one of the miracles of all time?"

Steiner, standing next to them, nodded. "Ah, yes. It must be so. As for me, I have seen this grow from its very origin, and I feel like a God to it. Yes, but perhaps not a very kindly God. We will probably have a little nebula on the edge of this universe tonight, after the silly little people blow up against our barriers. That is what I think will happen. They will go up in a puff of light, and then, *poof*—all will be much as it was before."

Warren stared into the pulsing mass of stars and sky, and asked, "Isn't there the slightest chance that they could break through? After all, they are concentrating a great deal of power against one small fraction of the skin of their universe. Might it not break open, release the disturbance into our own space-time, and close again?"

Marge sucked in her breath. Steiner chuckled. "There is a very slight chance that that could happen, yes. But luckily for us, it is not going to. If it did we might have a terrible explosion here, but the chance has been removed because we have our own atomic forces working to hold the universe in check. We do not rely just on this little universe's own borders; we never could. Left to itself, it would have expanded beyond our building. Of course now that it is falling back, it will not do that, but we are keeping our magnetic grip on it. And as long as our own outside forces are here, there will be no breakthrough, long chance or not. No, it will not happen."

He waved a hand around the balcony that edged the inner dome. Warren and Marge saw again the beams that focused upon the microcosm from all angles, above and below and around the sphere. "Is there a control here for these?" asked Marge.

Steiner nodded. "Yes, there is a small panel over there by the main telescope, but it cannot turn off the power. It can only modify it or intensify it for our own use. But it cannot be turned off. Only the failure of our atomic pile could do that, and the switches for that are in the powerhouse, not here."

So they stood there for a half hour, while night fell, and time moved on. They were silent, held as always by the marvel of the man-made universe. Once Marge asked, "Is anybody to be in transferal tonight?"

Warren shook his head. "Enderby thought it would be dangerous. It would have been interesting to have been on the break-through flight, but too dangerous. The chief thinks that it might affect the mind of the transferee. Besides, he said we can see what happened tomorrow. Those in the micro-universe who stayed behind will have pictures. If we can ever get them out of the mad-house that will be going on on the doomed worlds."

Marge shuddered. "I can't stand the thought. I would not go tomorrow. I do not want to go again into that universe."

Warren did not answer this. He understood her feelings very well. He stared into the microcosm. There, living and moving at a pace attuned to a different type of time and space, preparations were going on now for a climactic moment of life. Probably right now the break-through ships were gathering together, bolting down, piling up power vaster than any artificial construction had ever harnessed before, naming their commanders—surely the Oracle of the White Star, that strange eternal being, was among them—and beginning their trip to the farthest rim of their universe.

The clock on the wall registered ten. Marco, Enderby, and two others came in then. Gathering, thought Warren, like vultures for the prey.

Then from somewhere outside the dome there came the loud ringing of an alarm bell. They all looked up, stared at each other. Enderby, nearest the door, ran out into the night, suddenly stuck his head back in, and yelled, "Come on! There's a fight at the records hall!"

With one accord the great dome emptied. Warren and Marge and the scientists poured out through the door, and ran across the dark grass under the star-strewn sky. They could hear shouting, and there was a sharp report of a pistol.

There seemed to be a crowd of men milling around the records building. More men, thought Warren as he ran, than there were in the whole project. He heard a voice yell something, and with a start he recognized the voice of the guard Jack Quern, but the language was not English.

Plainly the spy had not waited. He had assembled his band, agents of some foreign power, and they had chosen this moment to descend in force, to raid the records hall and carry off those files whose information would make their possessor the most powerful nation for years to come—the very keys of the stars lay in those files.

There was a confused melee around the hall. Warren got a glimpse of helicopters standing on the grass, their great vanes idly turning. Then the spies had landed from the air; they were already in the records hall; men were trying to run out, burdened down with file cases.

He caught a glimpse of other men charging out of the trees, saw revolvers in their hands, heard shouts in English. The FBI had indeed staked out the place. There was a shout from one of the helicopters and an exchange of shots. Suddenly one of the strange planes burst into flames as a bullet struck its gas tank.

In the blaze of light from the burning plane, Warren caught glimpses of men locked in combat. He saw Stanhope lying across the door of the records hall, unconscious, blood smearing his face. It must have been he who had rung the alarm. Strange men were fighting in the doorway of the hall. Gray-haired Enderby and middle-aged Steiner were grappling with a mustached stranger whose arms were piled with files.

Warren punched blindly at another man who rushed at him. He felt the blow of a fist in his face, and he swung again, feeling his own fist crunch against the stranger's jaw. The other fell away, down and out. Warren looked around hastily to see what else he could do. Another helicopter was burning and now through the door of the records hall he saw a red flickering.

"Fire!" he yelled, but in the fight, none heard him. In a few more seconds, there was a burst of brilliant flame and the records hall was ablaze.

The men retreated from the glare, and the fight seemed over. Obviously this was a second objective of the spies; if they could not themselves possess the secrets, then they'd destroy them before others could make use of them. And in this objective they were succeeding.

Warren looked wildly around as he saw the strangers were fleeing. There would be a chase in the woods all night he knew, but they would not escape. Not any of them. He saw Marco frantically searching the grass in the flickering red light of the flames, salvaging whatever he could of the files that had already been taken.

Suddenly the thought occurred to Warren that he had

not seen Marge. Where had she been during this fight? Had she been hurt? He looked around, but he did not see her.

He wondered what time it was. The breakthrough attempt was almost due, but nobody would witness it. Had she started back to the dome, or had she been struck down in the brawl?

Frantically he looked about, then spotted the figure of a woman running toward one of the darkened buildings. It must be Marge, he thought, and ran after her, calling her name.

In the light of the fire, the girl turned her head to glance at him, but continued running. He set out after her.

She reached the squat cement building that housed the atomic pile. Warren saw her fumble at the door, saw it swing open.

He ran on after her, and the light went on inside the powerhouse. He got to the door. Inside it, the girl had run to the bank of controls that regulated the output of the pile, the dials that registered its flow and current. She was frantically searching over the mass of dials.

"Marge!" he called again. "What are you doing?"

She did not answer him. Instead she began hastily pulling plugs from their sockets, and finally found a master switch high up. She reached for it, and Warren started across to her, shouting, "Marge, stop!"

But she pulled the switch.

Inside the powerhouse the lights went out. She had cut the outlet between the pile and the rest of the buildings on the project. Outside all the lights went out, those in the main lodge, in the other buildings, and on the road.

The fire was still raging in the records hall and it is doubtful if anyone noticed the electric failure, what with the shooting in the woods, the seizure of the remaining helicopters by the rescuing guards and the general turmoil.

Warren reached Marge, intending to try to reconnect the

control board in the darkness. The girl grasped his arm, pulled him away. "Come outside, quick!" she said. He was pulled off balance and found himself following her to the door of the powerhouse.

Outside was a weird vista of flickering red shadows on the dark buildings, the moving silhouettes of men, the round rising dome of the dark hemisphere that housed the microcosm. Above them the sky was brilliantly clear and the stars shone down in mountain-air splendor; and the wide white band of the Milky Way was a road across the heavens.

"Watch the dome," said Marge in a breathless voice and her fire-lit white arm pointed at it. Warren stood transfixed, staring at the dome, wondering. It must be eleven o'clock, his mind noted with surprise.

"The power is off," whispered Marge. "There are no restrictive bonds on their universe. They can do it—I *know* they can do it!"

Before he realized just who she meant by "they," he was struck dumb. For there a sudden beam of light flashed from the top of the dome. It seemed to bore through like a single beam from a suddenly opened window—but there was no window or opening there.

Now a sudden vibration shook the air, an eerie ringing, singing note, and he saw the white beam widen, then break into many beams. This was followed at once by a rising excruciating pitch of sound, then an odd, almost noiseless puff that made his eardrums hurt as if pressure had suddenly been put on them.

He saw a little silver sliver shoot up the beam, a tiny splinter of metal. Then another and another, and still more. And the splinters of silver were rising into the sky, growing bigger as they rose, swelling into the air and the sky of the starlit night.

Now a whole cloud of splinters burst from the top of the dome, like a stream of sparks from a mighty log cast on glowing embers. As these splinters rose they grew, and it could be seen that they were ships—great silvery ships that rapidly expanded as they raced upward into the night sky.

In a little while it was over, the beam was gone, the night dark again, save for the dying embers of the burning records hall. There was a memory in Warren's brain of great dark shadows against the sky, of the stars being blotted out by the shapes of a strange armada of vessels that seemed momentarily to darken the sky from horizon to horizon before vanishing into the glowing vastnesses of the Milky Way.

Marge and Warren stood silent until the last shadow on the stars had disappeared from sight and the night was quiet again.

"They made it!" said Marge triumphantly. "I told them they'd make it! I promised them a new universe, an infinite universe, and now they're saved."

Warren turned to her, "*You* promised them?" he whispered, puzzled. "*You?*"

She turned her face to him, the light of the infinite stars in her eyes. "I was here to help them. I, alone."

"I don't understand," said Warren, still staring at her. "Who are you to help them? You are Marge McElroy, and your place is here. Where's your camera?"

The girl looked at him, her face glowing. "I'm Marge McElroy, now and forever. But I was also someone else. I was she who was known as the Oracle of the White Star."

Warren shook his head in confusion. "How could that be? The Oracle was a hundred women in succession, a hundred alien women."

Marge smiled. "I became the first Oracle and she was a brilliant woman, a true genius. She had the most powerful mind of them all. It was she who transferred her mind back to me here; it was her mind that occupied me, that trained me to think and see things as they were, and it never transferred back. The Oracle was in two places at once.

I was Marge McElroy and at the same time I kept the mental phasing with whoever was the Oracle. I never lost contact.

"You see, while you and the rest were spying in the microcosm, I was their spy here. The Oracle of the White Star was always I. What Marge knew, she knew—and her knowledge spanned a hundred generations, because I was always there."

She smiled, and shook her head. "But now it's finished. Somewhere on one of these ships an Oracle of the White Star rides. But she's no longer psychic; I've lost contact with her. She is no more the Oracle, but just a confused mystic whose influence will soon fade.

"Well, so be it. I've given them a new and greater universe, and now they can spread out and live in all its wonder and marvels. Nothing is lost of our records. . . . Because the real living records are up there, and when the time comes, we'll meet them and become part of them.

"As for me," she turned to him, "my life is here on Earth. We know of the things that have gone up in smoke on this mountain, Warren. Will you help me now to make a future for us both?"

Warren looked at her and he did not see any deep-eyed Oracle with bulging brow, nor an eternal priestess with miraculous insight. Instead he saw the sweet smiling face of a young girl, vibrant with youth, whose eyes had witnessed glory even as had his. And without further thought or unnecessary conversation, he simply bent down and kissed that face.